The sound of bugles . . .

Within seconds, the entire west wall opened fire. The fifty and thirty caliber machine guns were doing a job on the ranks of the Viet Cong assault force . . .

As the VC reached the wire and the smaller weapons began to have some effect along with the machine guns, the communist advance seemed to hesitate.

Whirling about, he grabbed up a scope and scanned the area to the southeast of the camp. The sick feeling in his stomach solidified like molten lead cooling as he stared, not wanting to believe, at what had to be nearly a battalion of Viet Cong. "I knew it! Those bastards are going to hit both walls at once!"

THE SCORPION SQUAD

BODY COUNT

Eric Helm

PINNACLE BOOKS   NEW YORK

THE SCORPION SQUAD #1: BODY COUNT

An original Pinnacle Books edition, published for the first time anywhere.

First printing/August 1984

ISBN: 0-523-42290-3

Can. ISBN: 0-523-43294-1

Cover art by Bruce Minney

Printed in the United States of America

PINNACLE BOOKS, INC.
1430 Broadway
New York, New York 10018

9 8 7 6 5 4 3 2 1

THE A-TEAM

CAPTAIN MACK GERBER	American A-team Commander
FIRST LIEUTENANT JONATHAN BROMHEAD	Executive Officer
MASTER SERGEANT ANTHONY B. FETTERMAN	Team Sergeant
SERGEANT FIRST CLASS IAN McMILLAN	Senior Medical Specialist
STAFF SERGEANT THOMAS JEFFERSON WASHINGTON	Medical Specialist
STAFF SERGEANT SULLY SMITH	Demolitions Expert
SERGEANT MILES CLARKE	Demolitions Expert
STAFF SERGEANT GALVIN BOCKER	Communications
SERGEANT SEAN CAVANAUGH	Communications
SERGEANT FIRST CLASS JUSTIN "BOOM-BOOM" TYME	Light Weapons
SERGEANT FIRST CLASS STEVEN KITTREDGE	Heavy Weapons
SERGEANT FIRST CLASS DEREK KEPLER	Intelligence Specialist

LLDB (LUC-LUONG DAC-BIET) A-TEAM

CAPTAIN TRANG	Commanding Officer
FIRST LIEUTENANT MINH	Executive Officer
SERGEANT HINH	Team Sergeant
SERGEANT TRI	Medical Specialist
SERGEANT TAM	Medical Specialist
SERGEANT VO	Demolitions Specialist
SERGEANT SUONG	Demolitions Specialist
SERGEANT LIM	Communications
SERGEANT LUONG	Communications
SERGEANT PHUOC	Light Weapons
SERGEANT DUONG	Heavy Weapons
SERGEANT TRAN	Intelligence

TAI TRIBESMEN

LIEUTENANT BAO	Company Commander
SERGEANT KRUNG	Tai NCO

BODY COUNT

PROLOGUE_____

REPUBLIC OF VIETNAM,
MEKONG RIVER DELTA,
MAY 1964

Sitting on the highest point in the immediate region, three men in dirty black pajamas were eating their morning breakfast of a couple of rice cakes. Nuyen Van Vinh swallowed a mouthful of water and stared at his two young companions. They hadn't been around long enough to be annoyed at the assignment. Scout the area for government troops. There hadn't been government troops here for fifteen years. And when there had been, those troops were French.

By the graying of the sky in the east, Vinh knew that the sun would be up in a little while. He screwed the top back on his canteen, which had been taken from a French soldier years ago. He leaned back so that he could stare at the rapidly fading stars.

They patroled into an area where there was no chance that they would see the enemy. The enemy was afraid to venture into this area. Vinh knew that he would never see a government soldier here.

He was right. He never would.

From somewhere came the quiet drone of a single-engine airplane that sounded like the noise of an overgrown insect. Vinh sat up and searched the heavens but didn't see anything. But the sound grew louder as the airplane came closer.

Then, just to the north, he thought he could see it. He

1

picked up his rifle, an old semi-automatic that had been taken from the same French soldier who had ''volunteered'' his canteen. Over the years, Vinh had lovingly cared for the weapon, until the bluing of the barrel was worn silver and the wooden stock shone like highly polished mahogany. He wondered if he should shoot at the airplane. No one had told him what to do if they saw an airplane.

The two youngsters were yelling excitedly and gesturing at the sky. Vinh shrugged, as if to tell them that he didn't really care what they did. He had been fighting for too long to get excited about one airplane, especially a tiny propeller-driven airplane.

The airplane passed overhead once, turned, flew over again, turned, and dumped the nose. There were two bright flashes under the wings and a second later the ground near them exploded into flames.

Vinh dived down, rolling to his stomach. To his right, he could see the body of one of the young men. His clothing was on fire, but he wasn't moving. Vinh knew he was dead.

Suddenly, from the east, came the roar of jet engines. As they dived for the hilltop where he lay concealed in the tall, thick grass, Vinh wondered how they had spotted him. Then he wondered why they would waste all that effort to kill him.

It was his last living thought.

The ground under him erupted and burst into flames as the first of the large napalm canisters hit. They were followed closely by others, and the four American jets began the process of clearing the top of the hill for the Green Beret camp that would be built.

The pilots never knew they killed the first three of many who would die on that hill.

CHAPTER 1 _____

REPUBLIC OF VIETNAM,
THE MEKONG RIVER DELTA,
MAY 1964

One morning there were nothing but occasional clumps of elephant grass and patches of tangled jungle scattered among the rice paddies and never-ending swamp south of the Parrot's Beak.

And Charlie.

The next morning there were three hundred sweating, groaning men and two large, bright yellow D-9 Caterpillar tractors busily chopping, chain-sawing, and bulldozing, a steadily growing circle of more or less level terrain from the top of a large, low hill that nevertheless remained the highest point in the surrounding countryside.

The air force had started the clearing operation at dawn with a mixed load of high-explosive bombs and napalm. With luck, the men would finish the clearing in two days' time and get on with the more important task of building, which had already begun in a primitive way with the two platoons of men who were filling and stacking sandbags.

U.S. Army Special Forces Captain Mack Gerber paused from his labors to wipe the perspiration from his forehead and survey the activity going on around him. He couldn't suppress a thin smile.

"Surprise, Charlie. You don't own the delta anymore."

"How's that sir?" asked a voice from behind him.

Gerber's executive officer, First Lieutenant Jonathan Bromhead, had come up the hill while Gerber was studying the broad flood plain, which stretched away to a series of low hills that more or less marked the Cambodian side of the border. Bromhead's dark green jungle fatigues were almost black with sweat. He was as thoroughly soaked as if he had been caught in a rainstorm. He eased his pistol belt and harness to the ground, pulled what was probably the only dry piece of cloth in the whole camp out of the combat pack attached to his pistol belt, and began wiping imaginary moisture off his heavy M-14 rifle.

"I was thinking how ~~pissed~~ off old Victor Charlie must have been when he woke up this morning and found out we'd decided to set up shop in his backyard."

Bromhead was suddenly serious. "You think the VC already know we're here, sir?"

Gerber smiled down at the freckle-faced young lieutenant who had not yet seen his twenty-third birthday. "This whole area has been a Viet Cong stronghold and sanctuary ever since the French paras and Legionnaires left Indochina in 1954. I think it's safe to assume that precious little goes on around here that Charlie doesn't know about. Besides, the flyboys weren't exactly gentle when they played reveille this morning."

Bromhead looked at Gerber sheepishly. "I see what you mean, sir. How much time do you figure we've got before Charlie starts taking an unhealthy interest in us?"

"We're probably under observation right now. I would think we've got between maybe three or four days and say a week at the outside before the VC can get their act together and organize a large enough force to really hit this place, but they aren't going to let any grass grow under their feet. Time is our ally, not Charlie's, and he knows it. The longer he waits, the stronger we get. Right now, a couple of good companies could push us off this hill. In a couple of days, we'll be able to hold off a regiment. He knows it, and we know it. The only question is which of us will be ready first." He paused, then added: "Was there something particular you wanted to talk about, Johnny?"

"Nothing important, sir," said Bromhead, getting to his feet and picking up his equipment. "I think I'll go see how Sergeant Kepler and his crew are coming along with the barbed wire."

"Good idea. Tell Derek I want two barriers of concertina around the whole compound by dusk, then find Sergeant Smith and tell him I want a ring of claymores between the wires by 1800 hours. Tell Sully to get Sergeant Clarke to help him if he needs it. And find Sergeant Schattschneider and tell him to start setting some trip flares up just inside the outer ring. Tell him to ask Lieutenant Minh to detail a couple of his men to help him. And Johnny, tell Sergeant Schattschneider to be sure and ask politely when he talks to Lieutenant Minh, okay?"

Bromhead grinned broadly. "Yes sir. I'll tell him to be sure and say please and thank you."

"One more thing. I want a team meeting at 1830. After that, I want everybody to stand to until one half hour after dark. There's no sense in having people wandering around the compound at dusk, providing an easy target for some smart VC sniper."

"Does that include the strike force, sir?"

"That includes everybody, Lieutenant. Especially the strike force. The Tais won't be any trouble. They're good troops and will do the right thing if you explain it to them. I'll speak to Captain Trang about our esteemed Vietnamese allies."

"Right sir."

Bromhead trotted off to his assigned tasks, and Gerber wearily trudged toward the main section of the camp where he could see his Vietnamese counterpart, Captain Trang, reposing comfortably in a folding canvas chair beneath a gaily striped parachute canopy awning, sipping at a tall glass of iced tea and reading a French novel.

"What a war," muttered Gerber. "I wonder where the little crook got the ice?"

Captain Trang was typical of many Vietnamese officers in the Luc-Luong Dac-Biet, the Vietnamese Special Forces. The LLDB* captain had obtained his commission through political connections with the powerful Roman Catholic Ngo family, which had ruled South Vietnam from 1955, after the departure of the French colonial government, until the recent coup headed by General Duong Van Minh. Under President Ngo Dinh Diem, nearly all officers in the Vietnamese army, navy, and air force had been political appointees, and the LLDB had been an elite unit, used primarily by Diem as a palace guard and as terrorist police. Diem had allied the LLDB with the U.S. Special Forces advisers in order to get the best equipment and training. As a result of the insistence by the American advisers, the LLDB had been forced to assume a greater role in counterinsurgency operations against the communist Viet Cong. Most were careful to send only their junior officers and NCOs out on patrols, which always ran the risk of being shot up by VC ambushes. It wasn't that they were cowards, exactly. They simply considered themselves too valuable to the Saigon government to put their own lives in unnecessary jeopardy. Many of them were financial opportunists as well. While some made big money in drugs or prostitution, most simply took advantage of kickbacks on government contracts and occasionally dabbled in Saigon's thriving black market. They did not view themselves as corrupt officers, merely as successful businessmen.

I guess maybe Trang really isn't so very different from some of the minor politicians and bureaucrats in the New York or Chicago political machines back home, Gerber mused as he approached the rotund little captain. I'll give him this much. He's got real political savvy. He came through the coup smelling like a rose.

---

* A glossary appears on page 210.

"May I speak with you a moment, Captain Trang?" said Gerber when he was within hearing distance of the Vietnamese officer.

Trang ignored him until he had walked up to the edge of the awning, then carefully folded the book in his hand and lowered it into his lap. He did not rise from the chair. "Of course, Captain. My time is your time. What may I do for you?"

"Sir," began Gerber, "experience has taught us that the men fight better in combat when they are led by their commanders, and they work harder when their commanders lead them in their work. As your advisor, it is my duty to call this to your attention."

"What you say may be true of Americans, Captain," said Trang, unperturbed, "but in the Vietnamese army, an officer directs the actions of his men, whether in combat or in work. From this vantage point I can see all the work in camp. It is from here much easier to see all work being done and all that is needing to be done. I can therefore more effectively direct activities of all men under my command."

Gerber shrugged inwardly at the Vietnamese logic. "Yes. I see your point, Captain. I wanted to talk to you about the necessity of having all troops on alert after 1800 hours."

Trang made a dismissive gesture. "Men all tired. All my men, they work very hard today under much sun. Tonight they must rest. Work hard again tomorrow."

"But our camp is a long way from being secure. If the Viet Cong attack us tonight, and no one is on alert, we could lose the camp and many men."

"VC not attack," Trang insisted. "VC not attack anything in this whole area for maybe five, maybe six years. Maybe longer. This is silly place to build base. Any VC here don't like much fight. They all pacified VC." Trang smiled at his joke.

"Both you and I know that the only pacified VC are dead VC, Captain," Gerber continued. "And the only reason there haven't been any attacks by the VC in this area is because there haven't been any government troops here for them to attack, until now. Now we are here, and the VC will attack us. We should keep half the men on alert until midnight, and then full alert until dawn. That way the VC cannot surprise us. Also everyone should be in position, ready to fight, from half an hour before dark until half an hour after. That way no one makes an easy target for some VC sniper who could shoot a few men and then slip away before we could get a patrol out to deal with him."

Trang sighed, put away his book, and got up. "VC will not attack us here. VC do not wish to fight here. Besides, we have the high ground. If you will excuse me, I must go now and check on the progress of Sergeant Hinh and his men, who are building our team bunker."

Gerber followed the Vietnamese captain away from his circus tent, protesting the necessity of his plan. They had gone less then twenty meters when Gerber heard a dull plop to the northwest of the camp, followed twenty seconds later by a rattling whine.

"Incoming!" Gerber yelled at the top of his lungs, and pitched forward onto the ground. His warning was followed by a shattering explosion. A few seconds later, there was another rattling whir, followed by an explosion, and then, about five seconds after that, a third. Then all was silent.

"Just harassing fire," said Gerber, getting slowly to his feet. "They just want to let us know that they know we're here." He stared at a suddenly ashen-faced Captain Trang, who was staring at the top of the hill where his colorful sun shade had been only moments before.

The first of the incoming VC 60mm mortar rounds had landed precisely in the center of the orange and white canopy, utterly destroying it. Of Captain Trang's folding chair, French novel, and iced tea glass, there was no trace.

"Looks like you were mistaken about the VC not

attacking, Captain,'' said Gerber, doing his best to suppress a smile.

Trang ignored the barb. "All men will stand to one half hour before sunset until one half hour after. I will consider what you say about keeping my men on alert tonight. Now I must go check with Sergeant Hinh.''

Gerber thought it was nothing short of amazing how Trang's English improved when he was too excited to play the role of the dumb ARVN—Army of the Republic Vietnam— captain. His understanding of military tactics seemed to improve dramatically under stress too. As Captain Trang hurried to check on the progress of his men, Gerber eyed the smoldering parachute appreciatively.

"That,'' he said softly to himself, "was not only damned good shooting, the timing was perfect. If I could meet that VC mortar man right now, I'd not only shake his hand, I'd give him a three-day pass in Saigon. Talk about the right place at the right time. I couldn't have planned it better myself.''

For the first time in weeks, Gerber whistled happily as he walked away to check on his men.

By the time the American Special Forces A-team meeting was called to order that evening, Gerber was no longer whistling. Now that the camp was actually being manned and under construction, he felt an enormous release from the tedium of planning and replanning that had gone on these last few weeks, but he remained greatly concerned over the security of the camp and the safety of his men, both the Americans and the hundred and fifty Tai tribesmen that made up one of his three strike-force companies.

The other two companies had been drawn from Regional Forces, despite much protesting from the district chief. Although possessing a rudimentary knowledge of military weapons and tactics, they were a complacent lot, not much given to the rigors of daytime patrols and completely uninterested in patrolling or setting out ambushes after dark. Gerber assumed that many of them were VC sympathizers, if not outright spies, although he doubted if many were actually hard-core Viet Cong. That wasn't a reflection upon the RF troopers' characters, merely Gerber's realistic assessment of the situation. The Viet Cong had ruled this whole area for over ten years. The Regional Forces had simply learned to coexist with the communists. The RF guarded important installations and communications facilities, and protected district officials and those politically well-connected individuals who at least gave the appearance of loyalty to the Saigon government. The RF did not go out into the countryside. The VC, for their part, let the RF alone in the towns and cities, which after all, provided nice recreational facilities for them, and went about their business of controlling and converting the villages, hamlets, and farms.

Gerber put little faith in the performance of the RF troopers under fire. Further, the Regional Forces assigned to the camp were under the immediate command of the Vietnamese Special Forces A-team. This meant that Gerber and his American team members could only advise the Vietnamese Special Forces commander, Captain Trang, as to the disposition and employment of the RF troops, a frequently frustrating experience.

The Tais, on the other hand, were paid by and directly controlled by the Americans, a situation the Vietnamese did not like but tolerated since they didn't like the Tais anyway. If the crazy Tais, who were always eager to go out on patrol and kill communists, wanted to risk their lives, fine. The more patrols the Tais went on, the fewer the Vietnamese had to.

Gerber's knowledge of the unhappy political situation within his own camp heightened his concern that the VC might try to take the camp before adequate defenses could be prepared. His Tais were good fighters, but he had no illusions about being able to hold a less-than-half-finished camp with a hundred and fifty men.

"Well," said Gerber, when all members of the team

were finally seated, "the good news is that we've finally got this show on the road and we're putting up a camp where we can finally put the hurt on Charlie. The bad news is that if Charlie puts the move on us in the next couple of days, the hurtin' is going to be all over us. Let's have your reports on how things are so far. We've got to start some place, so let's start with the wire. Kepler, how about it?"

"We've got two perimeters of concertina out all the way around. Some of it is stretched pretty thin in a place or two, though. I wish we had more wire. I've also got some tangle foot out in the high grass at the foot of the hill, but not enough. What we really ought to do is burn it off anyway, so the VC won't use it for cover, and then mine the whole area. Also, I'd like to start running patrols and putting out observation and listening posts as soon as possible, sir. If we're going to hold this place, we need to start finding out what Charlie is up to, and I mean starting yesterday."

"I agree, Derek," Gerber replied, "but our first priority has got to be finishing the camp defenses. With that in mind, you can start running reconnaissance patrols tomorrow, with the understanding that I'll only authorize one platoon of Tais for manpower, and no night patrols until after we get all the gun emplacements in and a double row of concertina on both perimeters. If you can talk Lieutenant Minh into loaning you a few of his RFs, fine. Work up a plan for rotating patrols, and let me have it by noon tomorrow. I'll see what I can do about expediting the additional wire."

Gerber turned to his senior demolitions specialist, Staff Sergeant Sully Smith, a short, stocky individual with a dusky complexion from Dayton, Ohio. Smith's real name was Francisco Giovanni Salvatore Smith, an unlikely combination that was due to his being the offspring of an army-air force flyer attached to the OSS in Trieste, Italy, during World War II, and one of the local maidens. A rebellious youth who had rejected his parents' Catholicism and preferred wild country to city dwelling, he had joined the army on his eighteenth birthday, an interservice transgression that his father, a career air-force officer, had still not entirely forgiven him for. At twenty-one and a half years of age, he had already completed one tour of duty with U.S. Special Forces in Vietnam and, after a brief leave stateside, had volunteered for a second tour because, in his own words, "I guess I just like blowing things up."

"How are you and Miles doing with the claymores, Sully?" asked Gerber.

"Coming along nicely, sir. Sergeant Clarke and I have one ring of M18A1s completely surrounding the camp, just outside the inner wire. We tied the mines together in groups of four with detonator cord and ran the leads back to the command bunker. We've also put out two dozen M-2 bounding mines between the wires, about ten meters up from Sergeant Schattschneider's trip flares. Sergeant Clarke and I are working on improvising some more bounding mines from a couple of dozen extra flares we got from Sergeant Schattschneider. We've put together some hollowed-out wooden blocks carved down to the right-size cylinder; we can put an M-26 frag in each one. The cylinder will fit nicely inside an M-48 trip-flare case, and the flare case holds the safety lever of the grenade in place after the pin is extracted. When the trip flare is initiated in the normal manner, the propellent charge fires the grenade into the air, and the spoon flies off. Detonation height is about ten meters, with considerable dispersion of fragments. The system isn't quite as effective or convenient as a regular M-2, but we had to improvise. Sergeant Vo, the LLDB senior demolitions specialist, apparently didn't load all the mines he was supposed to for shipment out here from B Detachment. I'm sorry, sir. I should have supervised the loading myself. It won't happen again."

"No point in worrying about that now," said Gerber. "I'll put in a request for more mines when I ask Colonel

Bates for Derek's extra wire. Could you use some more claymores too?''

Smith grinned. ''I can always make use of some more claymores, sir. Also, I could use about fifty pounds of number-ten spike nails. A hundred pounds would be better, if you can get them, sir.''

''What on earth for?'' Gerber asked.

''Well, sir, it's like this. About the only thing I've got a real surplus of is some one-pound TNT demolition blocks. Since it doesn't look like we're going to be blowing up too many bridges around here, I figured that if we had some spikes, Sergeant Clarke and I could tape a row of nails along the top and one side of the blocks, tie them together with det cord in groups of threes and fours, and use them to augment our existing claymores and mines. We will, of course, need some additional electrical tape, and half a dozen or so more rolls of lead wire. I've got plenty of electrical blasting caps.''

''Of course,'' said Gerber, stunned. ''Is there anything else you need?''

''Well, sir, I could use some powdered or flake laundry soap, say a couple of hundred pounds.''

''You want two hundred pounds of laundry detergent?'' said Gerber slowly.

''No sir. Soap. Detergent doesn't work right. I'm not a chemist, but it's not the same thing. If you can't get that, liquid dish soap or candles would be okay. Or I could use about twenty pounds of powdered lye drain cleaner and a hundred and fifty pounds of rosin or castor oil.''

''Sully, just exactly what do you have in mind?''

''Napalm, sir. I scrounged ten gallons of rubbing alcohol from Sergeant McMillan. Mix it with soap or wax or with the lye and oil or rosin, and some gasoline, and it produces a very passable gelled fuel. We can use ammo cans for containers, string them along the concertina, and command-detonate them with claymores or demolition blocks. Makes a very nasty surprise for anyone trying to come through the wire.''

"Sully," said Gerber, "I'm beginning to think you're a very nasty person."

"Thank you, sir."

"How's the infirmary shaping up, Doc?" Gerber asked Sergeant Ian McMillan, the senior medical specialist.

"Fine, sir. Sergeant Washington and I have been getting excellent help from our Vietnamese counterparts. You do have to watch them around the antibiotics and morphine, but other than that, they're not a bad lot."

McMillan shrugged. "I guess you have to expect that sort of thing, with the black market in drugs being what it is. Anyway, we've got cots set up to handle eight bed cases, and room for about the same number of litters, if necessary. I'd hate to have to operate under these conditions, but it'll do until we can get a more permanent cement structure. I do hope that won't be too long, sir," he finished pointedly.

"So do I, Doc."

"Bocker, how are we doing in the commo department?"

"Like Sergeant McMillan, we'll make do until we can arrange something more permanent. We've got plenty of PRC-10s to go around, and the long-range antennae are up on poles. Once we get the fire control tower up, we'll move the long-range stuff to the top of that, and use the pole setup as backup. We've a good supply of batteries for the man-portable units, and the long-range transmitters and receivers have been wired to draw power from the main camp generator if the independent generator fails. The backup independent generator hasn't arrived from B Detachment yet. We can also operate the long-range equipment off storage batteries for up to forty-eight hours if necessary. Sergeant Cavanaugh, with the assistance of Sergeant Clarke, has rigged destruction charges for the long-range radios, the generator, and the storage batteries in case the camp is overrun. Any additional equipment we have to leave behind can be destroyed by thermite grenades."

"Fine." Gerber turned to his heavy weapons specialist, Sergeant First Class Kittredge. "Steve, what's the word on the fire control tower?"

"We poured the pilings this afternoon, sir, but the construction people tell me it'll take two, maybe three days for the concrete to cure. After that, a CH-54 will fly the girder sections out from Saigon and lift them into place for us. In the meantime, we've set up a temporary twenty-foot tower on communications poles, using pallets for flooring, and sandbagging it. I don't think it would withstand a hit from a mortar but it should weather small-arms fire pretty well. With Sergeant Cavanaugh's help, we've run Lima Limas to the command bunker and each of the mortar pits. Sergeant Duong, my counterpart, is standing watch there now. He's a bit inexperienced but a fast learner. We've got a direction finder in up there, along with a range finder and a couple of pairs of naval binoculars I scrounged up before we left Saigon. We've also got an IR weapons sight up there for night observation, and, of course, a PRC-10, in case the telephones are disrupted.

"I've sited the mortars according to the plan I discussed with you earlier today. Right now, we've got six 60mm mortars and two 81mm mortars operational. I'd like to request that we ask B Detachment for another four of the eighty-ones and a couple of 4.2 inchers. That way we could use the 4.2s for illumination instead of the two eighty-ones we've got now. By freeing the eighty-ones and adding the four additional, we should pretty well be able to outreach Charlie's mortars, leaving the 60mms free to deal with the VC close in, when the assault comes.

"Working with Sergeant Tyme, we've sited a .50-caliber machine gun in each of the four corner bunkers, and a 75mm recoilless rifle in the center bunker of each wall. The bulldozers were a great help in getting the walls up fast and digging out the bunkers, but we haven't had time to get out pungi stakes yet. Sergeant Schattschneider's crew did get some out on the west wall, but the rest is pretty blank. We plan on rectifying that first thing in the morning.''

"Justin, what's the word on the rest of the weapons?''

Sergeant Tyme was a tall, sandy-haired young man from Philadelphia, in his midtwenties. A normally quiet man, he was at times, Gerber thought, almost overly serious. He was the team's light weapons specialist, and lived, breathed, and slept small arms. As far as Gerber knew, firearms was his only passion in life.

"Well, sir, you already know about the fifties and the seventy-fives. I've sited a .30-cal. Browning on each side of the recoilless rifles, on the north, south, and east walls, each halfway between the recoilless bunker and the corner. I also put two BAR teams on the north and south walls, since they're the most narrow, and three BAR teams on the east wall. That leaves the east wall a little bit thin, but I figured it the least likely route of approach. There's nothing out there but rice paddies, and Charlie doesn't like moving across that much open ground. I put the heaviest concentration of firepower on the west wall, facing the border, four BAR teams and four thirties. I also put two 3.5-inch rocket launcher teams out there.''

Gerber nodded his approval but could see that Tyme was not satisfied. "Have you any specific recommendations for enhancing our defensive capability, Justin?''

"Yes sir. More of everything, sir. We all know Charlie is going to take this base as a personal affront, and do his damnedest to kick our tails out of here. The BAR is a good weapon, but the twenty-round magazine puts a real limit on it in the sustained fire mode. We ought to have at least six more thirties and three or four fifties. The BARs are better suited to use on patrols or for ambushes. An extra fifty on each wall would double our capability to engage the enemy with long-range heavy automatic-weapons fire. We really ought to have two more fifties on that west wall.

We're not going to be getting any artillery support way out here, so we've got to rely on the air force, and you know what kind of proposition that can be, sir, particularly where the VNAF is concerned. As such, the more mortars we can get, the better. Also, I'd like to push for some more direct fire weapons. Rocket launchers are okay, but they're not really antipersonnel weapons. What we need are some more recoilless rifles, and I don't mean those 57mm jobs MAAG is always trying to palm off on us. The fifty-sevens are too heavy for patrol use, and don't pack a big enough punch anyway. We need some 90mm ones, or even a couple of 106s. What we really ought to have way out here is a couple of 105mm howitzers, but I suppose that's out of the question. We don't have the trained personnel to handle them anyway.''

"All right. I'll see what I can do. Some of the stuff you've asked for isn't going to be any problem. But you all know what the score is. MAAG controls the logistics, and some of those people still don't believe we're really fighting a war here yet.''

Gerber nodded at the team operations sergeant. "Okay, Bill, you're the last. Let's have the overall camp picture.''

"Yes sir,'' said Schattschneider. "You've already been briefed on the defensive aspects, so I won't belabor that. The construction boys spent most of the day doing general clearing and helping us get up the packed earth walls and dig the bunkers. Concrete has been poured for the fire-control-tower pilings, and for the foundations for the permanent commo and command bunkers. As noted, it's going to take awhile for it to cure before the structures can be completed.

"Tomorrow, the construction unit will be leveling and grading the runway through the middle of the camp. The strip will be twenty-two hundred feet long. That's kind of short, but it should be enough for U-1s and CV-2s, and it's all the hill we've got. We wouldn't have that much if they hadn't pushed the top off this hill and used it to fill in at the ends. That also runs the strip damned near up to the walls at either end. I'll give those navy Seabees one thing, they're a hardworking lot. I think they're anxious to get out of here before the real shooting starts. Especially after those mortar rounds we took late this morning.'' Schatt-schneider finished with a grin.

"Okay. How about general troop readiness, and E and E planning?''

"Well, the Tais are ready. The RF Vietnamese I'm not so sure about. They spend about as much time goofing off as they do working, and there's a few of them that I don't think know which end of a rifle goes toward the enemy.'' He shrugged. "I guess they'll learn fast enough when the shooting starts.

"As for escape and evasion, should it be necessary to evacuate the camp, I've selected two low hillocks, one to the south of the camp, toward the river, but not too close, and the other to the east-southeast. That one means crossing a lot of open ground, but it's big enough for a couple of helicopters to get in at the same time, is away from likely avenues of enemy approach, and we'll probably be using it at night anyway. North of the camp, there is one fairly clear area where a helicopter could get in and land on the road as a last resort. That's about it for now, I guess.''

Gerber leaned back in his folding metal chair and scratched at the stubble beginning to sprout on his chin. "Right. From now on, we're going to stand to from half an hour before dawn and dark to a half hour after. I want everybody on fifty-percent alert after dark, full alert after midnight. I don't really expect Charlie to try anything tonight, but I don't aim to give him the opportunity of an easy victory. I could only get Trang to agree to a fifty-percent alert for the Vietnamese. I guess he was afraid he'd lose his beauty rest. At least we'll have Lieutenant Minh and the best of his bunch after midnight, and, of course, the Tais. I want the eighty-ones ready for immediate illumination, and Sully, I want you to show both Lieutenant Bromhead and me just exactly how you've got those claymores wired up. Sergeants Schattschneider and Kepler will please remain to discuss plans for the night LPs. The rest of you work out a schedule and go get some sleep. That's all.''

As the men filed out of the bunker, Gerber couldn't help thinking about what Tyme had said about the lack of artillery support. It was true. If the VC were able to mount a large assault against the half-finished camp, the Special Forces men, without support, would be caught between a rock and a hard place.

Just give me a week, Gerber prayed silently, that's all I ask. One week, and Charlie will never be able to push us out of here.

Even as he thought it, he knew that it was a futile hope.

CHAPTER 2 ————————————

Lieutenant Colonel Alan Bates stood in the outer office watching the clock. The master sergeant sitting behind the scarred desk watched it too, and when it snapped from fifty-nine past the hour to 0900, he said, "You may go in now, sir."

Bates didn't need any further information because he had been doing the same thing every day, including the weekends, for the last three months. He stepped to the door, knocked, waited an instant, and then opened the door. Inside, Brigadier General Billy Joe Crinshaw sat behind his massive wooden desk writing. Bates knew better than to interrupt the general, but he also knew that Crinshaw was making him wait to show him that he was still the boss. There was no reason for it, because Bates was there at exactly nine every morning.

Finally Crinshaw looked up and said, "Okay, Alan. What do you have?"

Bates moved to the map and was mildly irritated that the intelligence specialist hadn't been in to update it yet and that Crinshaw was leaving it uncovered. Although Bates couldn't see how the distribution of enemy forces marked on the map would help the enemy since they themselves already knew where their soldiers were, the map was "secret" and should have been covered. Instead of saying anything, Bates opened his briefing folder, a leather case

20

embossed with the emblem of the Military Assistance Command, Vietnam, called MACV by everyone including the too-numerous reporters sent to learn the "real story."

"The overall situation hasn't changed significantly since yesterday's briefing. Units operating in the Iron Triangle area report no significant contact in the last twenty-four hours."

As was his habit, Crinshaw interrupted. "What do you call significant contact?"

Naturally the question was worded backward. Rather than telling the general what he meant by "insignificant," which he could easily have done, Bates had to explain nearly the whole situation. "Significant contact would be a platoon-size operation. There has been sporadic fire that has been quickly neutralized. The ARVN units had no trouble isolating the snipers. They killed two and captured a third. We believe that a large VC force was in the area, but by the time the ARVN got there, Charlie had plenty of warning. The snipers were only a harassment attempt."

Crinshaw nodded and said, "Continue."

"River patrols along the Mekong say that the amount of traffic is down since the last week. They believe that the VC have begun to collect taxes on the sampans and that they have discouraged travel. Now the locals are stopped, not only by us, but by the ARVN and the VC. There has been no confirmation of the VC activity."

Bates pulled the page out of his folder and set it on the table near him. "Contact has been reported in the Cu Chi area, near Song Be, and at Hue. All this was merely mortar attacks of three or four rounds, or harassing fire by snipers. No one has reported any casualties in the last several hours.

"Other than that, General, there is nothing new to report. A complete briefing will be in your box by 1300."

"Thank you, Alan," said Crinshaw. "Anything else?"

The moment of truth had arrived. Bates closed his folder and said, "We put the beginnings of Camp A-555 in at dawn about here.'' Bates turned to the map and pointed to an area just north of the Mekong River near the Cambodian border.

Crinshaw raised his eyebrows and snapped, ''Why there? We've seen no significant activity in that area.''

Bates wanted to scream; they had been over this several times and Crinshaw always insisted that the camp could be better placed. But Bates, as the B Detachment commander, with help from General Hull, had won the day. Now Crinshaw wanted to go over the ground again.

Bates said, in an even voice that barely suppressed his anger. ''We've no reports from the area because we have no one in the area. It has been a VC stronghold for years. The ARVN won't operate there because it's too far from Saigon, and local support, if there is any, probably feels abandoned by the government. Why should they stick their necks out? All Charlie does is collect a few taxes of rice and fish and draft an occasional male. And he guarantees that the war won't come to their homes. Now, suddenly, there is a government camp right in the middle of the area and Charlie can't do anything about it, yet.''

''But there are no reports, Colonel,'' insisted Crinshaw.

''No sir, there are not. Except for the scouting report from the A-team intelligence sergeant and the heavy-weapons sergeant who went in a couple of weeks ago. They reported that they had seen quite a bit of evidence of VC activity.''

''All unconfirmed by any other source.''

Bates was becoming exasperated. No matter what he said, Crinshaw had an argument against it. All he could do was agree. ''Yes sir. But we thought enough of the reports to continue with the operation.''

Crinshaw picked up his pen and tapped his chin with it as if thinking. ''I wish we had consulted more on this. It would strike me that the camp should have been located closer to Tay Ninh.''

Bates looked at the map and realized that Crinshaw

wanted something nearly fifty miles from where they were. Bates didn't have to keep explaining it because all the orders were cut, the operation approved, but Crinshaw, who controlled a lot of the supplies, could cause a lot of trouble if he wasn't appeased. So Bates said, "Yes sir. However, we have a couple of teams in that general area and they've been getting out to the surrounding countryside. This new camp is just what we need."

Now it was Crinshaw's turn for anger. "All right," he snapped. "What has happened so far?"

"Not too much. Air force planes napalmed the area, establishing, or rather enlarging the clearing. Less than an hour later, after the fires had burned down, we used helicopters to land men and supplies. Right now, about three hundred and fifty strikers, with one A-team, are there, trying to build a night laager for immediate defense as they rush to finish the camp. Everything should be in place in a matter of days."

Crinshaw got up and walked around his desk. He idly touched the brass bottom of a 105mm artillery shell that was now an ashtray. "I just don't like this. The resupply routes are all easily interrupted. One road and the Mekong River. Charlie can plug either anytime he wants."

"We can resupply by air. Helicopters can get in there anytime. I think resupply is the least of the problems."

"It's going to be a major problem, Colonel. I wish you had thought this out a little more carefully. There are twelve men whose lives are at stake."

"Plus the Vietnamese," Bates reminded him.

"Damn the Vietnamese. If they had any guts, they wouldn't have let their country get into this mess."

Although he could have pointed out that it wasn't totally a Vietnamese problem, reminding Crinshaw of the history of the region would do no good. All he could say was "Yes sir," and let it go.

"And that doesn't even include the equipment that you're going to need to establish that base," continued Crinshaw.

It's going to be a real drain on our resources." He slapped the map, almost as if the gesture could wipe away the new base.

Bates nodded but didn't trust himself to say anything.

"You can see that, can't you?"

"I can certainly see where it will require that we divert some of our resources to cover it." The answer was noncommittal. There were things Bates wanted to say, such as that the new base was doing the job that it was supposed to do, and Bates could wonder that Crinshaw planned to do with all the material. It was supposed to go to the units in the field. Crinshaw seemed to be hoarding supplies. Bates really just couldn't see what Crinshaw was upset about.

Crinshaw moved to his high-backed leather chair and sat down. He pointed to one of the chairs opposite him. "Alan, I think we might need to have a little talk."

Bates picked up his briefing folder, made sure that all his papers were there, and then made a production out of covering the map. Finally he sat down and looked at Crinshaw, waiting. Behind Crinshaw was a number of captured VC weapons, each mounted on a board like a game fish, and each inscribed with a brass plaque that gave the details of its capture. Crinshaw had appropriated them from an operations major by telling him that such mementos would have an undesired effect on his promotion opportunities.

"Alan," said Crinshaw by way of preamble, "I think that we may have a bit of a problem here. Placement of that camp was determined outside this office, and I don't like that. We have had quite a few reports of VC activity in the area that I suggested. We've seen convoys, convoys with trucks, damm it, drive across the border in the vicinity of Tay Ninh. I brought all this up, but you and your General Hull choose to ignore it."

"We didn't ignore it, General." Bates stopped for a minute and wasn't going to say more, then thought better of it. "We'll be able to block your infiltration routes once this camp is established. It all worked into an overall plan to put our people into areas where Charlie has had a free hand for years. It all—"

"You're missing the point, Alan. If I didn't know better, I would think you're being deliberately obtuse. I'm saying that you have not been a team player. We could have arranged a compromise, but you insisted on dragging General Hull into this. That has done nothing for the prestige of this office. You must remember that."

At once Bates understood the problem. It wasn't the actual location of the camp, but the fact that he had gone outside to get it located there that irked Crinshaw. The general wouldn't have cared if it had been in China, if only Bates had not consulted with Hull. Trying to soothe Crinshaw, Bates said, "But General Hull asked. There was nothing I could do about it. I certainly wouldn't have taken my problems outside the chain of command."

Crinshaw smiled for the first time. "I see. Well, we'll just have to be a little more careful around some of these chairborne commandos here, won't we?" Crinshaw gave him a conspiratorial wink.

To himself, Bates said, *you included*, but to Crinshaw he said, "Yes sir. They all want to stick their fingers in the pie."

"I'm glad that we understand each other."

Bates checked his folder, as if he was ready to leave. He said, "I'm sure we do, General."

Before Crinshaw could respond, there was a loud bang, like metal slamming against metal, and the air conditioner wheezed to a halt. Smoke poured out the vent and Crinshaw dived for the plug, yanking it from the paneled wall. For a moment there was silence, and then Crinshaw said, "Damm it. I told them I needed a new one. I'll probably have to wait all day for a replacement."

Bates moved to the door and mumbled, "War is hell."

Crinshaw looked up from the field phone set on his desk and asked, ''What was that, Alan?''

''Oh, nothing sir. I was just commenting on the general sloppiness of the troops these days. Can't seem to get anything right.''

''You said a mouthful, boy. A mouthful.''

CHAPTER 3 _____

CAMP A-555

Sixteen hours after Crinshaw and Bates finished arguing over the merits of placing Special Forces Camp A-555 in a region with no hard intelligence of enemy activity, Team Operations Sergeant Schattschneider died.

It might be said that he died because he jumped the wrong way, but the simple fact of the matter was that Master Sergeant William Henry Schattschneider, Jr., or the Third—Schattschneider himself had always claimed that he was never exactly sure which one he was—was merely in the wrong place at the wrong time. He left behind a wife and three children in Fayetteville, North Carolina. He also left behind a mortgaged house, a half-paid-for station wagon, and little else besides his government insurance policy.

He died while on his way to take over one of the camp's two key 81mm mortars. The base had come under rocket and mortar fire from the west, toward the river and the Cambodian border. An incoming mortar bomb had landed near one of the eighty-ones and wounded several members of the crew, temporarily knocking the mortar out of action. Gerber, seeing this from his position atop the command bunker, had called the 60mm mortar pit that was Schattschneider's station and told him to take over the eighty-one and get it back into action. The irony was that Schattschneider had misunderstood the order and run toward the wrong pit.

As he approached the emplacement, the mortar crew fired another round. Startled by the flash from the mortar tube, Schattschneider had risen up from his running crouch in order to better see into the pit. As he did so, a Soviet-manufactured 140mm rocket burst nearby, killing him instantly. It is doubtful he would have lived even had he been wearing a helmet, which he was not. William Henry Schattschneider, Jr., or the Third—now no one would ever know which—was not found until almost twenty minutes later by the A-team's assistant medical specialist, Staff Sergeant Washington. Schattschneider was sprawled flat on his back near the mortar pit, a look both quizzical and perplexed upon his face, his wide open eyes staring blankly up at the star-studded Southeast Asian sky, a jagged piece of shrapnel protruding from his brow. He was thirty-two.

Earlier, following the team meeting, Gerber had argued with Kepler and Schattschneider over the over the composition of the teams to be sent out to man the listening posts beyond the outer perimeter.

Gerber had wanted to keep all the Americans within the camp the first night to man key defensive positions, but Kepler had pointed out the need for having trained personnel in the LPs, men capable of assessing the strength and direction of enemy movement. He had also pointed out the tendency of the Vietnamese to resist strongly the desire to go outside the camp, any camp, after dark, for any reason, and the general lack of experience and fighting spirit among the Regional Forces soldiers. The Tais, although unquestionably brave, and excellent fighters, did not yet have a high degree of military training, and tended to overestimate numbers of the enemy when they encountered Viet Cong. Captain Trang had insisted that all the LLDB team members remain in camp, pointing out that their mission was, after all, to defend the camp, and his men were more qualified to operate the heavy weapons of the camp's defenses than were the Tais or RF troopers. What he neglected to mention was that remaining in camp also incidentally put them in a better position to protect him.

Schattschneider had sided with Kepler in the debate, and in the end, Gerber acknowledge the logic of the intelligence sergeant's position.

At 2130 hours, Gerber saw the three teams selected to occupy the LP sites Kepler had scouted earlier in the day go out through the wire and bamboo gates in the concertina. Kepler led one team of four Tais which would occupy an LP sited in a broad band of trees that paralleled a bend in the river southwest of the camp. Sergeant Tyme led another team of four to a position near a small wooden bridge that extended across the river from the road north of the camp, the road itself running on across the border before disappearing into the hills on the Cambodian side. Although the road had shown signs of frequent use, no traffic had been observed since the Green Berets had moved in that morning and started building their camp. The final team, which would occupy a small hill topped with a few trees among the rice paddies to the east of the camp, was composed entirely of Tais, and led by Sergeant Krung, whom Kepler had judged to be the best of the Tai NCOs.

Each team carried a PRC-10 backpack radio and trailed communications wire behind for a field telephone. In addition to individual weapons, there was either a .30-caliber Browning machine gun or a BAR in each team, and an M-79 grenade launcher with three basic loads of 40mm grenades.

Every man assigned to occupy the LPs carried six hand grenades and either an M3A1 submachine gun, or an M-2 automatic carbine with a dozen magazines of ammunition. Every man, that is, with the exception of Sergeant Tyme, whom, Gerber later learned, had taken a Remington 12-gauge pump shotgun and two-hundred rounds of number-four buckshot, in addition to the Belgian-made 9mm semi-automatic pistol he always carried.

Once they were in place, each LP team reported to the command bunker by radio and by field telephone, to ensure that both means of communication were working properly. After that, each LP checked in every half hour. Each LP, that is, except for the one manned by the Tais.

When the eastern LP failed to report, Gerber agonized over what action to take. He was reluctant to call them, for fear that a Viet Cong patrol might have stopped near the LP, and if he called, the ringer on the Tai's telephone, although muffled by tape, might give away their position to the enemy. At last he tried the radio, but the Tais were either unwilling, or unable, to answer.

When the Tais failed to report in the next half hour, Gerber resolved to try the field telephone despite the risk. Repeated efforts produced no results.

Gerber now became concerned that the Tai patrol had been ambushed. Although there had been no firing outside the perimeter and each of the three patrol leaders had carried a number of flares with instructions to fire one of a specific color if they were attacked (green for the Tais, red for Kepler, and white for Tyme), Gerber felt it unlikely that a VC patrol would remain camped next to the Tais' LP for over an hour. The Tais' excelled in stealth, and he did not think it likely the VC in this area would be good enough to sneak up on the Tais after years of coming and going as they pleased, but experience had taught him that almost anything was possible in warfare, especially when fighting guerrillas. Perhaps the patrol had walked into an ambush of crossbows, a favorite weapon of the Tais themselves. He didn't know. But he did know that one of his LPs had failed to report in twice in a row, and he had to find out why.

Summoning Lieutenant Bao, the Tai Strike Company commander, Gerber instructed him to take a patrol out into the paddies and find out what had gone wrong. Kittredge, in the makeshift fire control tower, reported he could see nothing through his infrared telescope. Gerber carefully briefed the short, wiry tribesman before Bao took a heavily armed five-man patrol out through the east gate to check on the silent LP. The mission was doubly dangerous. Not only was there the risk of running into a Viet Cong patrol, one which perhaps had already killed the LP team, there was also the danger that the Tais in the LP, if they were still all right, might fire on the patrol sent to check on them. Without communication with the camp, the men in the LP would have no way of knowing that a friendly patrol was approaching their position.

Bao was back in forty minutes, an exasperated look on his face. "Sergeant Krung say he turn off radio, disconnect phone," he explained to Gerber. "He say they make too much noise and VC not come close enough to kill. He say VC must come close, so his men can kill with knife. He say Sergeant Kepler tell him must be absolute quiet in LP, therefore he can no shoot VC, must let them get close and count how many. Sergeant Krung not like this. He say we come here to kill VC, not make game counting them. I tell Sergeant Krung when he count VC and report same every half hour, this help us to kill *beaucoup* VC later. Sergeant Krung still not like this, but I say many more guns in camp. Soon all guns shoot at VC, but first must count. I have to make promise to Sergeant Krung. I tell him he must do this American way, then soon Americans show him how to kill maybe twenty, maybe fifty VC. Sergeant Krung agree to count and report all VC he looksee. He much like Americans, much hate VC. Krung good soldier, good fighter, but sometime maybe not think so good because he hate VC too much."

Gerber knew that this was true. He had seen the tattoo on Krung's chest that said, "Sat Cong"—kill communists. The Viet Cong had, several years earlier, killed Krung's father, mother, and two brothers, and gang-raped his twelve-year-old sister. The Viet Cong had done this, they said, because Krung's father was the hamlet chief and had refused to help the Viet Cong in their struggle to liberate the people of South Vietnam from their oppressors in Saigon and their American lackeys. Such a fate, the Viet Cong patrol had said, belonged to all traitors who refused to help the Viet Cong.

Krung himself had escaped because he was visiting a friend in another village at the time. The sister had later committed suicide out of shame. When Krung heard of the incident, he had publicly sworn a vow not to rest until he had killed ten Viet Cong for each member of his family. According to Bao, Krung kept score by nailing the genitals of those he killed to a board he kept in his hootch. He was already halfway toward making good his promise.

Sergeant Krung, delighted at the prospect of killing perhaps as many as fifty Viet Cong, thereafter reported faithfully every half hour. The night passed quietly until two o'clock in the morning, when Tyme radioed that he'd heard splashing and what sounded like a boat being dragged up on the shore near the bridge. At exactly two A.M., the field telephone Gerber had dragged up on the roof of the command bunker rang. It was Krung, reporting that a group of three VC had slipped past his position fifteen minutes earlier, heading in the direction of the camp. They had been dressed in black pajamas and carried knapsacks. Sergeant Krung had not seen any weapons, but in the low light could not be sure whether the men had been armed or not.

Fearing Sergeant Krung had once again interpreted orders too literally, Gerber asked why he had waited until the regular reporting time to call the information in. The Tai explained that he had waited in order to make sure there were no other VC nearby. He had estimated that the enemy guerrillas would need at least fifteen minutes to reach the camp's outer perimeter because they were traveling slowly and with great caution. Also, he admitted, Lieutenant Bao had been explicit about the order to report every half hour. Given the situation, he had thought it best to wait, as he did not wish to disobey his lieutenant's orders, and he hoped more of the enemy might pass, so he could kill more VC when the firing started.

Gerber instructed Krung to report any further activity immediately, then called his executive officer, Lieutenant Bromhead, who was positioned in the central recoilless rifle bunker on the east wall. Bromhead had one of the camp's other two IR—infrared—scopes and had mounted the night sight on his M-14.

"Johnny, Krung's LP has reported three sappers heading your way," said Gerber. "There may be more. It looks like they're going to try and probe the wire. Don't overplay our defenses, but don't let any of them get away either. We don't want Charlie to know how easy it would be to take this place. Let them get in good and close, be sure of your targets, and then take them. It's likely some of the strikers on the wall will start shooting when you do, even if they don't have any targets, and when that happens, all hell will break loose. Don't use the seventy-five unless we're assaulted, and pass the word to the strikers to hold their fire unless they have something to shoot at. It probably won't do any good, but tell them anyway."

Bromhead acknowledged the order and passed along the word. He was little concerned about a few sappers probing the perimeter. After hearing Smith, Kittredge, and Tyme detail the camp's defenses during the team meeting, he did not share his CO's view that the camp would be easy to take, even though the defenses were incomplete. He did, however, understand the tactical sense of not displaying the disposition and nature of the camp's total firepower to the enemy. After scoping the paddies below with the IR light source switched off (to assure himself that there were no enemy snipers similarly equipped), he switched on the weapon sight's lamp. Through the eyepiece of the electronic telescope, the paddies sprang into instant yellow-green illumination—as did several intervening dikes, which

could conceal any guerrillas wading in the paddies themselves. Bromhead was not able to detect any movement.
He reported as much to Gerber.

At five minutes past two, Kepler reported that he had
heard several voices and the rattle of equipment south-
southeast of his position, in the treeline that followed the
river. He could not positively state which side of the river
the disturbance was on. The enemy did not seem overly
concerned with sound discipline.

Gerber had no more than hung up the telephone when
Tyme reported that he had heard movement and voices on
three sides of him. The enemy seemed to be moving
directly toward his position, and he told Gerber he intended to shut down his radio so as not to jeopardize his
location.

Gerber sent a striker to the LLDB team bunker to wake
Captain Trang and tell him that the camp was about to be
hit from three different directions, and that the American
captain advised that Captain Trang wake up the rest of his
men.

As the Vietnamese runner took off across the camp,
Gerber saw a bright flash south of Kepler's position and
heard the distant plop of a mortar round leaving the tube. He
immediately called the fire control tower nearby.

Kittredge had also seen the flash, but had not been fast
enough to get an exact bearing on it with the direction
finder. As he spoke to Gerber, the first round slammed
into the camp between the perimeters, doing little real
damage, and a crackling of desultory rifle and light machine
gun fire broke out from a low hillock directly west of the
camp. The range was far too great for the shots to have
any accuracy, and most of the rounds passed high over the
camp.

Kittredge got a plot on the tube flash as the enemy
mortar fired a second time and two of the camp's 60mm
mortars returned fire. As the VC mortar flashed a third
time, the rounds of the sixties exploded, bracketing the

enemy position. Kittredge immediately called for each of
the two mortars to fire four rounds of high explosive,
followed by four rounds of white phosphorus. Before he
could observe the results, there was a whooshing roar and
heavy enemy rocket fire began landing in the camp itself.
After a half-dozen thunderous explosions, there was a brief
moment of eerie silence, punctuated only by the thunk-
clang of outgoing rounds from the two sixties. Then the
silence was broken by the ugly ripping of heavy machine
gun slugs raking the northwest corner of the camp. It was
joined a second later by another salvo of rockets and a
final round from the enemy mortar across the river. As the
HE and WP shells from the sixties smashed into the treeline
on the far bank, the VC mortar fell silent and did not fire
again. The VC mortar men's aim had improved, however,
and the last of their shots had temporarily knocked out one
of the eighty-ones.

It was at this point that Gerber ordered Schattschneider
to take over the pit and get some illumination out over the
river where the rifle and small-arms fire was coming from.
Gerber had deliberately delayed using flares until now in
order to give Kittredge and Sergeant Duong in the fire
control tower an opportunity, when the VC fired, to spot
the enemy mortar, rocket, and heavy machine gun positions by their flashes and to get a bearing on them. He had
also feared exposing his LPs if the area was illuminated.

Schattschneider, misunderstanding the order, grabbed
his M-14, leaped out of his position in the number-three
60mm pit, and ran across the compound toward the wrong
eighty-one, and smack into a piece of shrapnel as the third
rocket salvo hit the camp.

While the master sergeant was sprinting toward his death,
Gerber had called the northwest corner bunker where Sergeant Sean Cavanaugh, the junior communications specialist,
was manning the key .50-caliber machine gun position,
and asked him if he could see where the rockets were
coming from.

"Yes sir," answered the nineteen-year-old sergeant. "It's set up right next to the heavy machine gun, but I can't fire. They must be sitting almost in Tyme's lap."

Gerber, seeing Schattschneider had not yet been able to get the eighty-one into action, called the number-two heavy mortar pit and told them to get some illumination across the river. This they did, and Gerber then advised Lieutenant Minh to have the southwest fifty bunker and the 75mm recoilless rifle sited in the middle of the west wall—both of which were manned by Vietnamese strikers under the direction of an LLDB sergeant—engage the enemy rifle and machine gun position. As the LLDB executive officer got on the telephone, small-arms fire broke out on the east wall. A second later, one of the trip flares positioned inside the outer wire went up on that side of the camp, indicating that the enemy was inside the outer perimeter. The whole east wall, and part of the south wall, immediately erupted in heavy firing. Gerber called number-two 81mm pit and told them to swing their mortar around and get some illumination out on that side of the camp. He then called Bromhead, who informed him that he had shot one of the three VC sappers who had slipped through the outer line of concertina after tying back some of the coils. The second man, panicking, had run forward, initiating the trip flare, and the whole wall, with the exception of the recoilless crew in Bromhead's bunker, had opened fire, despite the earlier warning to hold off. The east wall was manned primarily by the RFs, and the sight of the trip flare going up had been too much for them. Those who hadn't been cowering in their sandbagged revetment since the first mortar round had hit the camp, were sure the base was about to be overrun and had let loose, without any real targets. Bromhead calmly shot the second sapper with his M-14 before the glare of the trip flare had washed out the image in his infrared telescope. As the big flares from the eighty-ones had popped overhead, he saw the third sapper dash across a short stretch of open ground, drop back over a dike into a paddy and disappear, but was unable to get a decent shot at him through the fuzzy scope.

Outside the camp, Sergeant Tyme had his hands full. Sergeant Cavanaugh's description of the enemy as sitting in Tyme's lap had not been far off. Two groups of Viet Cong had moved in on either side of Tyme's LP, not fifteen yards distant. One group had set up a .50-caliber machine gun, which was now raking the camp, and the other, larger group, had set up launchers for the 140mm rockets. Part of the men then moved off, crossing back over the river, apparently to establish the position from which the rifle and light machine gun harrassing fire had come. They left eight men behind to fire and reload the rocket launchers and a four-man crew to man the machine gun. Tyme's five-man patrol was huddled in a shallow hole directly between the two groups of Viet Cong.

Realizing that the men in the camp could not return fire without the risk of hitting his position, Tyme signaled to his men, holding up two hand grenades. He pointed to each Tai in turn and indicated the direction in which he should throw: two men toward the rocket launchers, the other two, and Tyme himself, toward the machine gun. The division of targets had been simple. At such close range, it was vital to knock out the machine gun. The rockets, although making a mess of the camp, could not be used against Tyme.

Quietly, each man took two grenades from the pockets of his tiger-striped fatigues, removed the pin from one, and waited for the signal, holding down the safety lever of the grenade.

At Tyme's harshly shouted "*Go!*" all five men threw a grenade, yanked the pin from the second grenade, and threw it before hunkering down in the hole.

At the sound of Tyme's voice, the enemy suddenly stopped firing. A puzzled voice could be heard asking something in Vietnamese, and then the grenades went off

in a series of shattering explosions, sending shrapnel whin-
ing over the heads of the men in the LP. The men stayed
low, waiting for the second batch of grenades to explode.

As the last of the steel fragments whined away into the
night, amid the screams and curses of the wounded Viet
Cong, Tyme and his men leaped from their hole and
assaulted the enemy positions. Mixed in among the hammering of the submachine guns and the deep-throated chug-
ging of the team's BAR, Tyme's shotgun thundered twice.
Then everything fell silent, and Tyme and the Tais scuttled
back into their hole.

The first Viet Cong attack on Special Forces Camp
A-555 was over.

Back in the camp, Gerber was assessing the damage.
Six men had been wounded, the four Tais manning the
number-one 81mm mortar and two RF strikers who had
panicked and run out into the open during the initial rocket
barrage. None was seriously hurt, although three had to be
evacuated to Saigon because of the danger of infection.
Bromhead had finally gotten the strikers on the east wall to
stop shooting at shadows, and Captain Trang had at last
appeared, attired in helmet and flack jacket and carrying a
Thompson submachine gun and a whole knapsack full of
magazines. He was escorted by the LLDB sergeant, Thoung
Si Hinh, similarly attired, armed, and armored, and a
diminutive communications specialist, Trung Si Luong,
who was carrying only a folding stock carbine with a
couple of jungle clips, and a heavy PRC-10 radio. He was
hatless and wore a dark green T-shirt.

Gerber gave Luong an understanding smile. He felt
genuinely sorry for Luong, saddled as the man was with
such a pair for commander and team sergeant. Both Bocker
and Cavanaugh considered Luong—who had studied broadcast engineering in France before being drafted into the
ARVN and eventually finding his way into the Vietnamese
Special Forces—to be an exceptionally bright young man.

Unlike most LLDB members, he was not politically well connected, but had progressed on his own merits. He spoke both French and English fluently, was quiet, intellectual, and well liked by the Americans. Next to Lieutenant Minh, he was the most competent and professional of the whole LLDB A-team.

"More VC come?" Trang asked anxiously. "Maybe we need call B-team, get air support. Maybe we have to get helicopters, maybe evacuate the camp."

"I think that an evacuation might be a bit premature, *Dai uy*," Gerber said in disgust. "They just wanted to find out how serious we were about staying, that's all. It was a probing attack, nothing more. The shooting is all over. You're safe now."

The final barb was not lost on Trang, but before he could come up with a suitable reply, Washington came up to tell Gerber that Schattschneider was dead.

Shortly after dawn, the patrols came in from the night LPs, each team leader radioing that he was ready to enter the camp and popping a yellow smoke grenade before approaching the outer perimeter wire. None of the teams had suffered any casualties. Tyme's group came in lugging the .50-caliber machine gun that had been used by the VC in the attack the night before. The gun had not been seriously damaged, and it was repaired and used to augment the camp's defenses.

A short time later, a helicopter landed in the camp to evac the wounded, and to take Master Sergeant Schattschneider's body back to Saigon. Because an American had been killed, it was an army aviation helicopter instead of one from VNAF.

Krung's patrol was the last to come in. The Tai had a grimly satisfied smile on his thin lips. The third sapper, the one that had slipped into the paddies before Bromhead could shoot, had not gotten away after all. There would be one more set of genitals hanging from the Tai sergeant's scoreboard that night.

Tyme later took a patrol back to the area near the bridge and found a sampan that the Viet Cong had apparently used to cross the river with the night before. It was riddled with rifle fire and sunk.

That afternoon, the bodies of the fifteen Viet Cong soldiers killed during the attack were buried in a common grave dug by one of the construction crew bulldozers.

CHAPTER 4 _____

The day after the first mortar and ground attack—or rather, the first morning after the first day—it was decided that some kind of patrol needed to go out. Not a major recon, just a small operation that might pinpoint the enemy position and provide a clue about the size of the enemy forces in the AO. Gerber didn't waste a lot of time telling the men what to look for. Sully Smith and Derek Kepler had been in long enough to know what to look for. So Gerber just told them to be careful, to stay out no more than seventy-two hours, to pick the best of the strikers but to use some of the Vietnamese, and to have fun. And no, they couldn't take Lieutenant Minh, the British-trained officer, although he was definitely the best of the Vietnamese.

Just before dawn, and just before the first hint of light broke in the east, Smith led the fifteen-man patrol through some gaps in the wire, gaps that had purposely been left so that patrols could get out. Once clear of the wire, they wormed their way to the nearest road, not more than three-hundred meters from the last strand of the concertina, and stopped to lock and load. Smith had a superstitious fear of loading the weapons in camp before a mission. Since the Vietnamese tended to be slightly trigger happy, the other team members respected his superstition.

At the road, Smith jammed a twenty-round magazine

41

into his M-14, watched as Kepler did the same, and waited while the Vietnamese followed suit with their strange collection of rifles left over from World War II and Korea. Once that was done, they sent two men out for point, put a couple more out as flankers, and started off through the tall grass that could be hiding an entire NVA division. Except that Smith knew the VC weren't close because there was no sound, except for the night birds, and there was no telltale odor of nuoc-mam, the foul-smelling sauce used by the Vietnamese.

They spread out, keeping each other dimly in sight as the dawn began. Smith hoped to be several klicks from the camp before it was completely light. He planned to lie low for a couple of hours, just waiting and listening, in a modified ambush. He didn't expect anything, but it was the best he could do until the camp was finished and patrolling started for real.

After an hour, they turned to the northwest, keeping away from the trails and trying to keep quiet, but it wasn't easy in the swampy areas. They worked their way through light scrub brush, which rustled in the early morning breeze that helped mask any noise they made.

At 6:30, Smith began looking for a place to set his ambush. Charlie would be looking for a place to hide: at least, he would, if he was worried about the new camp. But Smith didn't think that Charlie was worried. He had owned the region for too long.

They came to a trail that showed recent, if not heavy use, and established a classic L-shaped ambush. Smith moved around it, checking the postions of the strikers, cautioning each of them to remain quiet and not to shoot until he ordered them to do so. Smith knew that they would never hear such an order because he didn't plan to give it. Knowing the Vietnamese, he figured that if he, Kepler, or the Tais began shooting, the Vietnamese would join in. Once everyone was in place, Smith set out a couple of claymore mines facing down the trail.

When everything was ready, he moved back around the ambush, telling each striker to take a drink of water now because later they weren't supposed to move. Any movement, no matter how slight, could give them away.

Finally, Smith found his own place, took his drink and salt tablets, and settled in. He could hear the sounds of small animals, but no other humans. Somewhere in the distance he heard the drone of an airplane, but he didn't look for it. He just sat still, watching the trail, hoping that Charlie would soon be moving along it.

He was mildly surprised when, less than an hour later, he heard sounds in the distance, sounds that indicated someone was beginning to use the trail. He turned his head slightly and concentrated. In a few minutes he heard more sound, and then voices. Charlie certainly didn't respect noise discipline, but then you never did in your own territory.

Smith leaned over and tapped the shoulder of the man nearest to him, nodded toward the sound, and signaled him to be quiet and patient. The word was passed.

Far off, there was a burst of laughter, and Smith knew that the enemy was getting close. He wasn't sure whether they should spring the trap or not. It wasn't that Charlie didn't know they were in the area, building the camp, but Charlie didn't know that they would be patrolling. If he sprang the trap, it would warn Charlie that they were out there.

Of course, it would be an interesting test of the discipline of the Vietnamese. Could they watch the VC walk by without shooting? Smith wasn't sure. He thought that this group might. Then he decided that it didn't matter. They were to look for the enemy, and the fastest way to find them was to have them looking for Smith. Spring the ambush, let Charlie know that they were around, and see what kind of trouble that caused.

Smith had made his decision none too soon. The head of the enemy unit appeared about two-hundred meters down the trail. Smith watched, hoping that it wasn't a company. Several more VC appeared, then a large group of fifteen or twenty clumped together. They weren't even following normal squad tactics, as if they didn't care because they were invincible. That was about to become a fatal error.

The enemy point man had reached into the kill zone. Now things would become tense. Smith hoped that Kepler, who was anchoring the other leg, would be able to control the strikers there. They had preached, over and over, that patience would be rewarded but the discipline so carefully instilled in the rear areas had a way of evaporating in the field.

Carefully, and quietly, Smith reached along the stock of his M-14 and made sure the safety was off. The point man was about halfway down the long axis of the ambush, and the group of twenty or so was entering the killing zone. Behind them was another ten, and farther back still a couple of stragglers: the rear guard. They were spaced far enough apart so that the point man would be outside the ambush by the time the last of them entered it. That couldn't be helped, and Smith figured that he could get him before he could get away.

As the last of the enemy entered the ambush, Smith reached over and detonated one of the claymores. The whole jungle erupted as a fusillade poured onto the trail. The enemy, caught in the open and by surprise, reacted with panic. Many stood rooted to the ground, unable to move. Others tried to run up the trail, toward the short leg of the ambush, and were cut down.

Smith turned and saw the point man fleeing toward a large clump of trees, most of his body masked by the tall grass. He squeezed off a dozen shots that sent the man sprawling. When Smith turned back, there didn't seem to be anyone living on the trail, but the Vietnamese were pumping round after round into the bodies. Smith ordered a cease-fire, heard Kepler doing the same, and slowly the shooting tapered off.

They waited a few minutes, to see if there would be any other enemy units that might be close, but heard nothing. Kepler had sent a couple of strikers down the trail as security. Finally Smith stepped into the open to check the enemy dead. Kepler followed suit, checking the bodies closest to him, working his way toward Smith. The strikers saw this as an opportunity to take trophies: things like ears and hands. Smith ordered them to stop, then told the ranking Vietnamese that they should leave the bodies alone and search for intelligence: documents, unit insignias, weapons, and anything else that might provide clues to the size and distribution of the enemy. The Vietnamese didn't like it and protested, but then Smith told them that it would scare Charlie more to find the remains of his unit this way, with no clue as to who had done it. They saw the wisdom and humor in this. Besides, the captured weapons were trophy enough.

When Kepler got close to Smith, he said, "Now what?"

"Let's move off nine or ten klicks and set up for the night."

"You think that Charlie will be looking for us?"

"I don't know. You can bet that someone heard the shooting, but I don't know what their reaction will be. Maybe they'll think it was target practice by someone. It's hard to tell how they will behave this deep in their own territory." Smith looked at the strikers who were forming up to move out. "About the only thing I can think of is that we should get out of here."

They started off down the trail, picked up the two guards, and then veered to the north, away from the trees and light brush and into the elephant grass that surrounded the few rice paddies in the region. As they moved into the open—the grass coming up to their waists in most places, but shoulder-high in a few—they increased the distance between them slowly, checking for signs of the enemy. But they didn't find much because Charlie had not felt the need to hide.

For an hour they walked down the long axis of a treeline, keeping to the shelter and moving slowly, looking for booby traps, pungi stakes, and mines. Charlie didn't mine the area, though; such a move would be self-defeating. Thus Smith knew that booby traps would work well against Charlie because he wouldn't be expecting them. Every three or four hundred meters he stopped long enough to hide a small mine or explosive device. He kept a log of them so that he could caution the rest of the team even though he was spreading them so thin that his caution didn't seem necessary.

He had just set a tiny mine near a tree when he noticed that the patrol had stopped. He inched forward and found Kepler staring into a large open area that contained a mud hootch, a broken-down, mud-fence corral for water buffalo, and a tiny bunker in the corner. The bunker didn't look as if it had been used recently, but the hootch had a metal roof that had only just begun to rust.

Smith leaned closer to Kepler and said, simply, "Well?"

"I would guess that it's just what it looks like. A rice farmer's hootch."

"So where's the farmer and his family?"

"Working the paddies, I would imagine, especially at this time of day."

Smith studied the area carefully and then asked, "So what do we do?"

"Nothing. Let's just move around it and not bother anyone."

Smith tapped one of the Tai strikers on the shoulder and pointed to the left, signaling that he should skirt the area, staying just inside the trees. As the man disappeared in the distance, the rest of the squad got to its feet and followed. They hadn't gone another five-hundred meters when they came to several dozen hootches clustered together.

Smith looked at his map, checked his compass, and shrugged as Kepler walked up. He said, "It's not on the map."

"That's no surprise. The map is twenty years old."

"One thing for sure." Smith laughed. "We know it's not a friendly village. Should we go in?"

"I think not. Let's just stay here and watch for a while. Might give us a clue about the enemy."

Smith got up, patted Kepler on the shoulder, and then moved back so that he could form the squad into a defensive perimeter. It would give the men a chance to eat and rest while Kepler studied the hamlet.

It didn't take him long. All he saw were old men and women and young boys and girls. Everyone who would have been of military age was gone. Kepler didn't know if they had been drafted or had volunteered. He did know, given the amount of activity, that there should have been some young people. Finally he slipped deeper into the trees and whispered to Smith, "I've seen all I need to. Let's get out and find a night location."

Silently, they pulled deeper into the trees and then walked off toward the Cambodian border. Two hours before sundown, they found what they wanted to use as a night laager. It was well concealed, was near a source of water, but not near enough to be bothered by animals—or by humans. They took it easy, that is, easy for a patrol, keeping only a couple of men on guard. Smith had decided to rest as much as he could early on because after midnight he planned on having all the men awake. He didn't expect trouble because he didn't think Charlie was used to having the Green Berets in his backyard. It would take a couple of days for it to sink in. Charlie's communication system wasn't as fast as the Berets', but he would soon be alert.

The night passed quietly. The only problem was a tiger that had strayed out of the hills. It came close but wasn't interested, and soon stalked away. With the morning sun, the patrol was ready to move again, having eaten breakfast—a couple of handfuls of wet rice—in the dark.

The new day was nearly a repeat of the last, except they didn't find any new signs of Charlie. Just more of the same. No young men or women, only the old and the very young. And signs that military operations had been conducted in the area, signs of movement of troops and equipment, and even a couple of abandoned bases, outlined by disintegrating bunkers. These bunkers hadn't been well built and hadn't been cared for. They were signs of Charlie's complacency, signs that he was at home in this area—signs that the job Smith and the A-team had to do was going to be a lot harder than they had originally thought.

They stopped at noon, rested for over an hour, and then headed south, more or less back toward the camp. But they were also moving toward the Cambodian border. They stopped in the middle of the afternoon, the hottest part of the day. Kepler watched, looked for signs of the enemy, but found little of interest.

They moved off again, looking for a night location, but discovered instead a well-used trail. Smith and Kepler discussed it, decided that since it was the last night, this would be a good place for an ambush. They had enough time to get it established before dark, feed the troops and then go on half alert. If nothing else, this would be good practice.

Smith surveyed the trail, found the best place for the ambushers, and then studied the trees opposite them. Standard U.S. Army tactics were to charge into the ambush, thereby confusing the ambushers and probably breaking it up. However, Charlie wasn't trained that way. Smith counted on him running from the ambush and taking cover on the other side of the trail. He scattered a couple of his mini-mines along the ditch and then placed two claymores so that they would rake the most likely hiding spots. His last claymore was placed so that it would fire at an angle, down the trail. That done, he eased back to anchor the short leg of the ambush.

Night came, and the sounds around them changed as the day animals hid from those of the night, but there was no sign of the VC. Smith listened carefully but could hear no noise from his troops. They had understood the importance of silence. The Tais were never any problem; they wanted to kill communists, but the Vietnamese sometimes refused to believe Smith or the other Berets when they were told that absolute quiet was necessary for the ambush to work.

Fortunately, just as had happened the day before, they didn't have to wait long. Long waits tended to make the men impatient and careless. They would shift position. They would lose interest, and then the enemy could sneak up and turn the tables.

And just like the day before, the VC didn't seem to believe that anyone would be around, so they still weren't observing standard field tactics. They were talking and smoking, and Smith knew of their approach long before they moved into sight.

This time the VC moved toward them in a large group, barely maintaining any semblance of a column. They were strung out over nearly seventy-five meters, which made their column longer than the long axis of the ambush. Smith didn't worry about this, especially since it was dark.

Just as the lead man was about to leave the ambush, Smith opened fire, killing him. Over the noise of the shooting, he yelled, "Fire!"—not because it was necessary but because he had to yell something.

The woods erupted as the rest of the team began shooting. The first few of the enemy dropped and there were several screams. But this time the shooting wasn't as good as it had been in the daylight because the Vietnamese tended to aim high. And Charlie didn't react like he was supposed to. Instead of fleeing into the trees on the opposite of the trail, the VC hesitated only a few seconds. One of them shouted something, and they charged forward, into the trees.

Smith watched one of the enemy seem to loom out of the dark in front of him. He swung his rifle around and fired without aiming. The enemy fell backward. But that was the only VC that Smith could see. The rest of them disappeared into the trees. Around him he could hear shouting, mostly in Vietnamese, and there was some shooting, but nothing like there would have been if Charlie had stayed in the open.

Smith didn't want to move. The claymore controls were in front of him, set on the ground in an order that told him which one would fire which. And with the enemy now in the trees with his strikers, it would be hard to tell them apart in the dark.

To his left he heard some movement. Carefully, he set his rifle down, the operating rod up so that the breech wouldn't be in the dirt, and pulled the knife that he had taped upside down to his web gear. By looking to the side, he could see a figure moving toward him. He couldn't see a helmet or hat, and assumed that the man there was an enemy. Smith waited for him to get a little closer and then reached out, grabbing him by the wrist and yanking him forward as he reached out with the knife, slicing into the man. There was a grunt as the VC died, and Smith let him fall.

At the other end of the ambush, Kepler wasn't quite as surprised to see the enemy charge their position. He reached for his grenades, pulled the pins, and tossed two of them onto the trail. He was sure that his own strikers, crouching behind the available cover, would be protected from the shrapnel. As he reached for his rifle, someone jumped him. Kepler rolled with the impact and tried to draw his knife. He lost his grip on it, found it again, and whipped it out as he heaved the man over his head. Kepler scrambled around, onto his hands and knees, and knifed the VC before he could turn.

Kepler clambered back to his position and picked up his rifle. He saw another man coming at him and fired as two more leaped out of the dark. Kepler felt a white-hot pain in his side as the enemy's knife ripped through the cloth of his tiger suit. Kepler dodged away and punched with his doubled fist. He felt his hand sink into soft flesh and heard the strangled grunt as if he had hit the enemy in the throat. He drew his arm back sharply and connected with the nose of the VC behind him, driving splintered bone into the man's brain and killing him.

Now he crawled forward, found his rifle, and yelled, "Open fire! Fire you stupid bastards!"

Suddenly the firing increased, as if the strikers finally realized that they had the advantage. The enemy had no protection. It was almost as if reinforcements had joined the strikers. The VC were confused, and although they outnumbered the patrol nearly two to one, their determination broke and they ran backward, to the trail and then across it.

Seeing that, Smith smiled to himself and triggered the claymore that was angled on the trail. If Charlie had thoughts of regrouping and charging, that ended them. Now he was only interested in getting to cover, and as they reached the ditch, the mini-mines began going off, and Smith triggered the last two of his claymores.

For a moment, the only shooting was the Vietnamese strikers, pouring a stream of bright red tracers across the trail until Smith and Kepler could stop them. The two slowly began to work their way from the ambush location to the trail, checking the enemy to be sure that they were dead, picking up the weapons, and counting their own troops.

They discovered that they had four dead and two wounded, including Kepler himself, who was now dizzy from loss of blood. Smith examined the wound, found that it wasn't deep, and said, "You'll live."

Smith ordered a couple of the strikers to move up and down the trail for security, while they finished cleaning up. Once they were convinced that there were no more living VC around them—Smith didn't believe that they had killed them all, but did believe the survivors had fled deeper into the woods—he organized the strikers into two-man teams to prepare stretchers. Within an hour they were ready to move. Smith wanted to put distance between them and any enemy units that might have been around to hear the firefight.

At two, Smith called a halt, exmained the wounded again to make sure that neither of them was in danger, and let the strikers rest. They had brought the bodies of those killed too. One reason was because the Vietnamese believed that a burial was necessary for the soul of the deceased, and they wouldn't support anyone who left their dead in the field. And second, it gave Charlie another mystery to deal with.

By sunup, they were close to the camp. Smith called another halt as the sun rose. When it was completely light, he radioed in that he was popping a green smoke, and that they would be entering the perimeter from the south. Gerber met them as they passed through the last strand of wire. He looked at the two wounded men and saw that neither was badly hurt.

Smith turned to the squad and said, "Weapons check in five minutes."

"After that, I'll want to see you for a complete debriefing," said Gerber. He moved to Kepler. "How bad is it?"

"Just a scratch, really."

"Let McMillan look at it. I'll be over in a couple of minutes to talk to you before the medivac gets here."

Kepler was astounded. "Medivac? It's just a scratch, Captain."

"I know. I know. But out here even a scratch can be bad. We've nothing for infections right now, and that's going to be our biggest worry."

"But Captain," protested Kepler, "You're already a man short. Now—"

"Don't worry about it. We've got a replacement coming

in later today. Bringing us some of the supplies that we've asked for.''

"Captain—"

"That's it, Sergeant."

Kepler knew instantly that the discussion was closed. Whenever Gerber reverted to military titles, it meant that he would entertain no more discussion about a subject. So Kepler just nodded his agreement, got his weapon, and headed for the tent used by the doc.

Gerber turned and followed Smith into the team house. "How'd it go, Sully?"

"We were awful lucky, sir. They just weren't expecting us out there. We surprised them at every turn. We might be able to get away with this stuff one more time, but then Charlie's going to be alerted. He'll either bring in some hard-core VC, or he'll start retraining the guys he's got here. Either way, we're going to have to get our people trained so that we don't make a lot of dumb mistakes."

"You make any mistakes?"

"Not really. We couldn't. Everything was too loose out there. Charles just wasn't prepared."

"Anything specific?"

Smith finished taking off his web gear, letting it fall to the floor. "I think Derek will have something for you. I mean, we just ran a patrol with a couple of ambushes."

"And managed to get shot up," Gerber reminded him.

"That kind of underscores what I was saying. Charlie wasn't ready, but he reacted in that second ambush like a professional soldier. Or rather, an American soldier, charging into the ambush. If his discipline had been a little tighter, we could have been in the hurt locker."

Gerber moved to the door. "Okay. Why don't you get yourself some food and a shower and write out a brief report. Something that I can send to Saigon proving that we are pursuing the war with great and successful vigor."

"Have it to you by noon, sir."

"Don't knock yourself out." Gerber laughed.

Gerber found Kepler sitting in a lawn chair sipping a beer while McMillan attempted to clean his wound. Kepler smiled up at him and said, "I don't know why I was complaining about a couple of days in Saigon."

"I don't either, Derek. It's got to be better than here." Gerber dragged an empty ammo box over and sat down. "Anything I should know?"

"Didn't see a whole lot. Signs of military activity, but since we don't have any history for this area, I don't know if it's significant or not. Did notice that there are no military-age young men around. That could be very significant. I would expect some, unless the VC have started recruiting everyone to keep us from getting them. That whole thing bothers me.

"And that last unit we ran into. I don't think they were VC. Reacted more like hard-core troops, but there weren't any uniforms. We grabbed what we could, but in the dark it's hard to see. Got a whole pile of papers off the first bunch. Thought while I was down in Saigon, I could run them over to the Intell shop and have someone there go over them."

"Sounds good. What about weapons?"

"Usual mixed bag. Everything from Russian-made to a Swedish K to some captured from ARVN. Nothing significant. I don't see a real buildup yet. That's not to say they couldn't begin one today. Basically, it was just like Charlie owned the area and knew it and wasn't worried about us. He will be now, so the patrols going out will have to follow noise discipline and squad discipline. Old Charles will not be caught with his pants down again."

"What else?"

"Really not much, Captain. The people didn't take any notice of us, but then we tried to stay away from them. If we owned the area, it would be called pacified."

"You mean the VC have that strong of a hold?"

"No sir. I mean that there has been nothing going on here so long that the people accept the VC. Now they're going to be caught between us. And they'll support the VC for a while, until we can prove that we're stronger and tougher, and it's better for them to have us here."

Somewhere in the distance they heard the popping of rotor blades. Gerber stood up. "I'll want a complete report when you get back." He smiled again. "That is, if we can lure you away from Saigon."

"Yes sir. Lure."

Five minutes later, Kepler was on the helicopter that was disappearing in the east. Gerber wished that he himself was on it. He wasn't sure that he wanted to be where he was. But then, he doubted that any of them did. And what he didn't know was that by late afternoon, he too would be on his way to Saigon.

CHAPTER 5 _____

The afternoon helicopter was now nearly forty minutes late. Gerber walked across the compound, around a small group of Vietnamese who were trying to stack sandbags next to the wooden frame that was going to be an antimortar bunker; it would protect the civilian families of the strikers when they arrived, and stepped into the commo bunker. In the dim light, he could see two Vietnamese and Sergeant Bocker working to reinforce part of one wall. Next to them was a radio, the tiny glowing lights on the panel told Gerber it was turned on.

"Chopper's late," Gerber said to announce himself.

Bocker turned. "Yes sir. Got held up at Trung Lap. Some hotshot colonel wanted a ride there and diverted the bird."

"Then there is nothing wrong?"

Bocker wiped his hands on this sweat-stained jungle fatigues. "No. Good news is that it's bringing in the new team sergeant. Some guy named Fetterman. Never met him."

"You got all that on the radio?"

"Yes sir."

"Pretty sloppy radio discipline on their part. Giving the names over the air like that." Gerber shook his head as if he couldn't believe the stupidity of the rear echelon commandos.

56

Before the sergeant could respond, they got another radio message. "Zulu Operations. Zulu Operations. This is Big Green."

Bocker answered. "Big Green, this is Zulu Ops. Go."

"Roger. Zulu Six is to report to Big Green Six at first possible moment. Repeat. Zulu Six is to report to Big Green Six at first possible moment. Understand that aviation asset is en route. Zulu Six is authorized to use it."

"Roger, Big Green. Understand Zulu Six to report immediately in person."

"Roger that. Big Green out."

Gerber shrugged and said, "Guess I better go pack." He had managed to keep the irritation out of his voice because he didn't want Sergeant Bocker to know exactly how angry he was. Without another word to anyone, he left the commo bunker.

As he crossed the compound, he could hear the drumming beat of the helicopter rotors in the distance. He hurried, not wanting to keep the chopper on the ground any longer than necessary. He doubted that Charlie would be in a position to do anything about it, but the longer it sat, the more time Charlie had to react. If they could get airborne in under a minute, then even if Charlie could fire at it, they could be gone before any mortar rounds hit the ground.

In his hootch, he realized that there wasn't much he needed. A change of underwear and clean socks. And even if he didn't take these, he could buy them in Saigon for about two dollars. He threw a couple of things into a knapsack, picked up this weapon, and headed out the door.

Outside, near the makeshift helipad, Gerber watched the helicopter approach. He turned and saw Sergeant Tyme pull the pin on a smoke grenade. Tyme tossed it to the center of the pad where it billowed purple smoke.

"Want me to bring you anything from Saigon, Justin?"

"No sir. Except maybe travel orders for the world."

Gerber laughed. "Yeah. Me too."

At that moment, there seemed to be a rattling just barely loud enough to penetrate the helicopter noise. The chopper broke to the right, falling toward the ground.

"Shit. They're taking fire." Gerber spun and raced toward the commo bunker. As he moved, he yelled at Tyme, "Get to the number-one 81mm pit. You know the approximate location of the hostiles."

Gerber ran into the commo bunker and grabbed a PRC-10. "Who is that in the chopper and what's their freq?"

"Crusader One-two on thirty-seven decimal five."

Back outside, Gerber turned on the radio, set the frequency, and waited for the tuning squeal to fade. "Crusader One-two, this is Zulu Six."

"Zulu Six, Crusader One-two. Taking fire about a klick north of your location."

"Roger. We saw it. Stay to the north so you don't foul the gun target lines and we'll hit it."

"Roger Six. ETA your location in about three zero. ID purple."

"Roger purple. Any other problems?"

"That's a negative."

Gerber reached for the field phone set near the door of the commo bunker. "Tyme, you can put three rounds of willy pete on the target."

"Yes sir. We don't have much of a chance of hitting them."

"I know. But let's let them know that we're here and we're going to shoot at them every chance we get."

"Yes sir."

Gerber waited a moment, watching the helicopter loop its way toward them and then begin its approach again. Bromhead ran out onto the landing pad and tossed another smoke grenade. To the left, he heard the pop of the mortar tube as the first of three rounds was fired. In rapid succession, there were two more, followed seconds later by the sound of the first round hitting the ground. Through the trees he could see the flash as the round exploded and the white cloud of smoke grew skyward. It looked like they had hit fairly close to where the fire had come from, but the distance and the angle could be deceiving.

Gerber stayed by the radio until the helicopter touched down. When it was on the ground, he shut off the PRC-10, handed it back to Sergeant Bocker, and ran over to the helipad, holding one hand on his beret to keep it from blowing off his head.

At the helipad, Tyme handed Gerber's knapsack to the crew chief, who tossed it under one of the seats, out of the way. Gerber stepped up so that he could talk to the aircraft commander, while Tyme and the crew chief tossed supply bundles out the door. When the young army warrant officer looked at him, Gerber said, "How was the trip in?"

"Only took fire from the one place. Piece of cake otherwise."

"Okay. Let's get out of here."

Tyme tapped Gerber on the shoulder and shouted over the noise of the helicopter, "Captain, this is Sergeant Fetterman."

Gerber turned to shake hands with the man. For a team sergeant, he couldn't have been more miscast. He was short, dark, and thin. Thin almost to the point of being skinny. With the helicopter pilot demanding that they leave, Gerber didn't have time to make a thorough study of his new team sergeant. He said, simply, "Welcome aboard. If you'll excuse me, I've got to get out of here. Lieutenant Bromhead will introduce you to the others and get you some quarters."

Fetterman merely nodded and said, "I understand, sir. See you when you return."

Neither man saluted because it did nothing other than identify the officers for the VC. Gerber was sure that the VC would be observing the camp, and probably already knew who the officers were, but there was no sense in giving them any help. Besides, his white skin identified him as an American, and that made him enough of a target.

The flight to Saigon was uneventful. They stayed far to the north of the area where the enemy had been so that they received no fire. Gerber tried to find out just how close the willy pete had come to hitting the enemy, but the AC refused to overfly the area, claiming that it was too late in the day, and if anything happened, no one would venture out to rescue them. Gerber was familiar enough with the command in Saigon to know that they would never approve a night mission to check the results of a couple of poorly aimed mortar rounds.

And he couldn't talk to anyone in the helicopter because of the noise of the engine and the ever-present popping of the rotor blades. All the crew members had helmets, so communications between the pilot and crew was possible. Since Gerber didn't have a helmet, all he could do was sit in the back, looking out the door, as the wet green of the rice paddies slipped by. Occasionally there was a village to break the monotony. But these were small, hidden in clusters of palm trees. Sometimes the only clue to their presence was the flashing of the tin roofs in the setting sun. It seemed so peaceful below. No five o'clock traffic, no smog from a hundred thousand cars. Nothing except the nearly empty landscape.

Gerber let his mind roam. If he didn't, he would be thinking about Crinshaw and the last thing he wanted to think about was Crinshaw. There would be enough time for that when he got to Saigon.

Gerber had no idea what Crinshaw wanted. He resented being pulled out of the field to answer a bunch of dumb questions but had been in the army long enough to know that you couldn't go kicking sand in someone's sandwich without getting into trouble. And he had kicked a lot of sand in Crinshaw's direction.

As it began to get dark on the ground, the aircraft began losing altitude and Gerber could see lights in the distance. They almost had to be from Ton Son Nhut, the main air base near Saigon. Gerber thought of it as an air base, although it was really Saigon's international airport.

They banked to the left, turning to the north. Gerber saw one of the main runways slip by. They seemed to gain altitude briefly, and then lost it all, coming to a hovering stop a couple of feet off the ground. A moment later, they touched down.

Gerber reached under the troop seat for his knapsack, grabbed his weapon firmly, and nodded to the crew chief. He hopped out of the helicopter and started across the grass, toward what looked like a terminal.

Before he reached the door, a tall, sandy-haired sergeant stopped him, saluted, and asked, "Are you Captain Gerber?"

"Yes."

"If you'll follow me, sir. General Crinshaw is waiting in his office to see you." The sergeant reached out, trying to take Gerber's bag.

"That's all right, Sergeant. I can manage."

"Certainly, sir."

They walked along for a few minutes, Gerber studying the surroundings carefully. It was the first time he had been to Ton Son Nhut. Somehow he always managed to miss it, except for the flight into Vietnam, and then he had been too preoccupied to notice much.

The sergeant recovered his jeep, waited while Gerber put his gear—except his weapon—into the backseat, and then drove off. As they turned a corner, the sergeant said, "We'll go straight to General Crinshaw's office. He's waiting. After that, I'll see about finding you some quarters for the night."

Gerber nodded.

*   *   *

In Crinshaw's outer office, a master sergeant behind an old desk sat doing nothing, other than watching the clock. When Gerber entered, the master sergeant told him to sit down. He picked up a field phone, spun the crank, and said, "Captain Gerber is here, General."

As he placed the handset of the field phone back in the cradle he said, "You can go in now, sir."

It was like stepping into a refrigerator. Gerber was sure that it wasn't more than sixty degrees in the room. The air conditioner was roaring away in the corner. Crinshaw sat behind his desk, working, and wearing a field jacket so that he wouldn't be cold. He didn't look up when Gerber entered the room.

Gerber wasn't sure what to do. Much of military courtesy was often ignored in the active units. In training everyone was always taught how to report, how and when to salute, and so on, but once out of the training environment, little of it was followed. Gerber stood for a moment, undecided, and then figured that a little grease applied now might save a little wear and tear later. He saluted and said, "General Crinshaw, Captain Gerber reporting as ordered."

Crinshaw dropped his pen, pushed his papers aside, and actually smiled at Gerber as he returned the salute. "At least someone in this unit knows a little about military protocol." He gestured to a chair. "Sit down, Captain, I have a few questions."

Gerber was mildly upset by the atmosphere in the room. He had expected a different reception. A hostile one. But Crinshaw was being too nice. Especially after the way he, Gerber, was summoned to Saigon. He sat down, set his beret on his knees, and waited.

For a few moments Crinshaw studied him from head to toe. Crinshaw saw a fairly young man, about twenty-eight or twenty-nine, who was six feet tall, had brown hair, and blue eyes. He looked tough—or at least he didn't have a potbelly that would have indicated a soft desk job—and it was obvious to Crinshaw that he worked hard at staying in shape. But then, most of the Green Berets did. Maybe a little too hard.

Finally, when the tension was almost palpable, Crinshaw reached to his left to pick up a piece of paper. He waved it at Gerber like some kind of banner. "Okay, boy. You tell me how you can be losing people at that base of yours."

Gerber didn't know what to say. For an instant he sat there, realizing that he would have to say something. Then, almost automatically, he said, "Enemy action."

"I don't think so. We've no Intell reports of enemy activity in the area."

"You may not, General, but we've been hit a couple of times in the last few days. Even the chopper that brought me in took some fire. Charlie is all over that area."

Crinshaw dropped his paper to his desk. He rocked back in his swivel chair and closed his eyes. "If that is true, then why are there no reports of enemy activity from that area?"

"Possibly because we haven't had anyone in there until now."

"That's the same kind of crap I've been getting from Bates. I just don't believe that Intelligence estimates could be so far off."

"They're not off, General. There aren't any. We haven't been there and the ARVN won't work there. It's just—"

Crinshaw waved a hand at him. "Shut up," he said. "Just shut up. I've had about all I can take from you people. I don't want any more losses in there. Is that clear?"

"But General—"

"Is that clear?"

"Yes sir. But how are we supposed to operate. If we run into the enemy, we're undoubtedly going to take casualties."

"You just don't get the picture, do you, boy? I've already had the ambassador in here. In here. He came to this office, and he wasn't happy. You're getting Americans killed out at that base, for God's sake. And I have to explain to him how you can be losing people out there when there are no reports of the enemy in the area.''

Gerber steeled himself and interrupted, realizing that it was something that he shouldn't be doing. Generals just did not seem to understand that the officers under them could think. ''There were the reports from a couple of my team members before we located the base. And I've brought with me an after-action report written by Sergeant Smith, explaining his contacts on a patrol we ran. They found two relatively large enemy forces in just two days. The VC, and possibly even North Vietnamese, are working there.'' He reached into the folder that he had brought and handed the report across the desk. Crinshaw ignored it.

''There are no corroborating reports. Everything is coming from your people who may be operating in their own self-interest. After all, you people selected the location of the base without any real input from this office.''

''Sergeant Kepler brought a stack of papers to Saigon. He has made his reports to Intelligence.''

''Still from the same source. Your people. You have to have some enemy bodies to show me. You don't have bodies, you don't have shit. You got that?''

''Yes sir.''

''I'm warning you, and you can tell your Colonel Bates, that I want confirmation of everything. If there isn't some confirmation soon, I'm going to take steps to get the base moved to a location that will be more useful. You had better be prepared to document everything. I mean documented and I mean everything. That clear?''

''Yes sir.''

''All right. Now get out of here. I've had enough of this for one night.''

Gerber stood, saluted, but didn't leave immediately. He was hesitating, wondering if Crinshaw wanted anything more. It seemed so unlikely that Crinshaw would pull him out of the field just to chew him out. But Crinshaw had picked up his paper and wasn't paying any attention to him. Gerber had already irritated Crinshaw enough for one day. He left the office, closing the door behind him so that none of the general's cold air would escape. The sweating master sergeant still sat behind his desk, watching the clock. Gerber shook his head.

At the door, Gerber stopped. "Is that all? Will the general want to see me tomorrow?"

"I'm sure that I don't know, Captain."

"Thanks."

Outside, the sergeant who had picked him up at the airport sat in the jeep, waiting. Gerber climbed into the passenger side and said, "What now?"

"My orders are to take you to your quarters and drop you off. After that, I'm free."

"Okay," said Gerber. "The general tell you anything about his plans for tomorrow?"

"No sir. Didn't the general tell you anything, sir?"

"No."

"Well, you should have asked."

"You're right there. I should have asked." They drove past a large building that was pouring light into the night sky. Over the door was a large sign that said OFFICER'S CLUB. Gerber tapped the sergeant on the shoulder and said, "Pull over there for a minute."

"Sir, all I'm suppose to do is take you to your quarters. Then I'm off duty."

"Don't worry, Sergeant. This won't take long. I just want to make a quick call."

Inside, Gerber found a field phone, somehow got the military operator for the base, and then, for his final miracle, managed to locate Bates. Bates said that he didn't know much about the trip, other than Crinshaw was pissed about everything and was doing all in his power to make life miserable for everyone. Bates concluded by saying, "Look, Mack, have a good time tonight. Have a steak. Drink a beer. And go back to your camp tomorrow. Don't worry about this. It's just Crinshaw's way of letting you know that he's in town."

"Okay, Colonel. See you tomorrow before I blast off."

CHAPTER 6

Just inside the door was a sign that told Gerber that he was required to leave his weapon in one of the boxes near the door. He didn't like that, especially since there was no way to lock the box, but the M-14 was just too conspicuous to carry in with him. It wasn't that he was worried about an attack. He was more concerned about someone stealing the weapon.

Gerber stored his weapon and then pushed open the second door, which led to the club proper. He saw a large room, hazy with cigarette and cigar smoke, crowded with tables and nearly three hundred people. A long wooden bar dominated one side of the room, and at the far side was another door. Over it was a sign that said GENERAL OFFICERS ONLY. Gerber smiled to himself and wondered why anyone would want to be alone in a room loaded with generals.

On the wall to the left was a giant black velvet painting of a matador slaughtering a bull, and under that was a brand-new jukebox blaring the latest hit tune. The jukebox took slugs, not coins, because everyone had to surrender his American money, exchanging it for MPC—military payment certificates—on entering the country. The alleged reason was to keep the greenbacks from flooding the Vietnamese economy. Gerber saw great possibilities for corruption in the slug-selling system. A bank of slot machines that also took slugs, located opposite the jukebox, confirmed this possibility.

Gerber walked to the bar and studied the rows upon rows of liquor bottles. He hadn't seen such variety or quantity in all the time he had been in Vietnam. At the bar, he asked for a shot of Beam's Choice.

The bartender, dressed in a Hawaiin shirt open to the third button, pushed him a glass. "That will be two bits."

Gerber downed the drink in one smooth gulp and pushed an MPC note at the bartender. "Two more."

"Yes sir."

Gerber drank those and then turned, leaning against the bar so that he could see the rest of the room. There was a stage in one corner, and a band was setting up. They were all in civilian clothes, and he noticed that they had a female singer. He knew that there were some USO shows around, but he had never seen one. And he knew that some of the enlisted men and embassy people put together bands to perform. He'd never been interested enough to ask anyone about it.

He turned back to the bar. "Can you sell me one of those bottles?"

"Yes sir. But you have to take it out of the club to drink it. I can only sell it by the drink in here."

"Okay. I'll take two of the Beam's Choice. And I want a beer."

"What kind?"

"Ah, make it Miller."

When he got everything, including his change, he moved away from the bar and found a table as far from the band as he could get. He set his green beret on the table, put the two bottles on the chair next to him, and sat down, sipping the beer. A young Vietnamese girl in a very short skirt came over and asked if he wanted anything to eat. He settled for a hamburger, rare, French fries, and another beer.

He sat there quietly, minding his own business, sometimes watching the antics of the people who never got out of Saigon. Like the men of his unit, the majority of them were young, but there were a few gray-haired men thrown in to look at them disapprovingly. Gerber just wasn't interested in any of them. They wouldn't be able to understand him and he certainly didn't understand them. Their attitude was reflected in Crinshaw. Somehow, Gerber felt, they should all be working together, not against one another. But Crinshaw seemed to think that there was some kind of game being played and they were on opposite sides—he jealously guarding his supplies, building his empire, and Gerber trying to get those supplies and undermine the empire.

He supposed it was something like the war being fought with the news media in Saigon. Gerber had already had a few requests for interviews about what he was trying to do, and had turned them down. He had talked to another captain, one who ran an A-team near Song Be. The man said that he had tried to be candid with the reporter, showing him everything, telling him how it really was, and the story the reporter wrote suggested that he, the captain, was a troublemaker who didn't understand. The story was spiced with quotes from colonels and generals from Saigon and the Pentagon who had no real idea about the war. Everyone was working against everyone else instead of cooperating. An incredibly stupid way to conduct a war.

And to make it worse, it seemed that the army was at war with the air force, and both were fighting the navy. At least on a policy level. At a working level, everyone seemed to get along. Gerber couldn't think of one bad thing to say about the Seabees, but knew that any recommendations for awards that he put them in for would be routinely rejected when they got to Saigon. It wouldn't look good for the army to be recommending the navy for medals.

Gerber drained the last of his beer as the hamburger

arrived. The girl put another beer in front of him as the music blasted out of the gigantic speakers set on the side of the stage. Gerber didn't recognize the song.

Just as he took a huge bite out of the hamburger, which was uncommonly good, he heard a voice to his left, trying to say something over the music. Gerber turned and saw a tall, thin woman with brown hair standing next to him. She was in a light, brightly colored dress. Gerber had never seen eyes so blue. He just stared at her.

She leaned close and said, just loud enough to be heard. "Do you mind if I join you?"

"Of course not." He smiled. He gestured at the chair opposite him, forgetting, for a moment his manners. He stood to pull it out.

"That's okay," she said. She sat down, saw the waitress approaching, and told her that she wanted a screwdriver. When the girl was gone, she leaned forward and said, "I usually don't do things like this, but you were all alone and I've had enough of all the so-called dashing fighter pilots chasing my tail. They just don't seem to understand that sometimes one would like to drink alone."

Gerber set his hamburger down and wiped his lips. "Well, I'll do my best to leave you alone." He said it seriously, but his eyes showed that he didn't mean it.

Apparently it was the right thing to say because she relaxed slightly. She held her hand across the table so he could shake it and said to him, "My name is Karen. Karen Morrow."

"I'm Mack Gerber."

Her drink arrived. She took a sip and said, "I always feel uncomfortable about that. Exchanging names. It never seems to go the way it should."

"I didn't think it was that awkward."

Gerber finished his hamburger and French fries. He drained the last of his beer and thought about leaving, but the only thing waiting for him was an empty room. Not a very comfortable one either, since he was just a captain and couldn't get up on the floors where the colonels and generals lived. He had thought about trying to find a room downtown, but it seemed to be more trouble than it was worth. If he was going to be there for a couple of days, it would have been a different matter.

Gerber ordered another beer and pointed at Karen's nearly empty glass. She nodded and he told the waitress to bring them one of each. As the drinks were placed in front of them, the band decided that it was time to take a break, and the noise level in the room dropped, making conversation possible. Gerber started it by saying, "What do you do?"

She looked at him and didn't speak.

Gerber thought about what he had said, and explained, "I didn't mean that the way it sounded. I meant, what is your job?"

She laughed. "I know what you meant, but the look on your face was priceless. I'm a flight nurse. In the air force."

"Stationed here?"

"No. Up at Nha Trang. Some general down here was having a party and invited a group of us down for the night. We get transporation back tomorrow."

"You left the party?"

"It was turning into an orgy. I didn't like the way the general and his cronies assumed that we would all be willing to fall into bed with any of them. I left. I don't think anyone really noticed." She pointed at his beret. "You're one of the Green Berets?"

"I'm not, but my hat is. I'm down here at the invitation of a general, I guess you could say. I didn't enjoy his party either."

"Are you stationed here?"

"Nope. Out to the west. On a small base."

She wanted to ask more, but had heard rumors about some of the missions the Green Berets were given and decided that it wouldn't be right. Besides, since his answer had been so noncommittal, he probably wouldn't talk.

Gerber picked up the ball again. "You get down here often?"

"Once or twice a month. You?"

"First time. But I think my general is going to have me coming in all the time to explain what I'm doing."

The music started again. Karen moved her chair closer so that she could talk. There were several couples on the dance floor. "Do you want to dance?"

Gerber thought about it. He had never really learned how to do the modern dances, but there didn't really seem to be much to them. He watched for a moment and then said, "Sure."

They spent an hour dancing to the poorly played music. Gerber couldn't say much for it except that it was loud, but no one seemed to care. Karen was having fun. He asked her, "You come here often?"

"You mean here, or Saigon?"

Gerber laughed. "I didn't really mean either. I was joking. You know, boy meets girls and asks her if she 'comes here often.' Sort of an opening line."

Now Karen laughed. "Okay, opening line. Here's one for you. Do you fool around?"

"I don't have to. I'm not married."

Karen stopped moving and stood looking at him as if she was stunned. Then she smiled broadly and said, "Me neither."

Gerber didn't know if she meant she didn't fool around or if she wasn't married and then decided that given the circumstances, it didn't matter. He just didn't know how things were going to turn out.

For nearly a minute they stood watching each other, then Karen leaned close to him. "Want to get out of here. I know a good place. It's a little quieter."

Gerber nodded and then headed back to the table to get

his bourbon and beret. They stopped long enough for him to recover his weapon and then stepped into the muggy night.

"You'll have to leave your rifle somewhere," Karen said. "You can't take it downtown."

"Okay, but the only place I have is my room. If you don't mind a stop there.",

"I don't suppose you have any civilian clothes?"

"No. I only had about ten minutes to prepare for the trip and I didn't plan on an evening out."

Outside the gate, they grabbed a cab, letting several lambrettas go by. Karen argued with the driver about the price of a ride to Cholon, the Chinese section of Saigon. As they rode through the streets, Karen explained that Cholon was the best area in Saigon, and there was a club called the Deadwood that reminded her of a bar in her hometown. It had a jukebox, but it was kept turned down so people could talk.

The Deadwood was everything that Karen had claimed. Dark, quiet, spacious, and comfortable. They sat opposite each other at a small table, leaning close so they could talk. They both had drinks, but didn't touch them often. They were just too interested in each other to notice much around them.

Finally, about midnight, Gerber said that he should be getting back. He had to be ready early. As he said it, he realized that Karen should be telling him that she had to go. He smiled about the irony of the situation.

Karen said, "Let's go then. We can find a cab outside."

Back at Ton Son Nhut, Gerber said that he would walk her to her quarters, and was mildly surprised when she asked if she could have a nightcap.

"Certainly. But I must warn you, once I get you alone in my room, all bets are off. You might be attacked."

"Promises. Promises."

Upstairs, Gerber learned that he was not staying in a hotel. There might be sheets on the bed—cot, really—and there might be towels in the bathroom (that was shared with a room on the other side) but there were no glasses. There were no paper cups. There was nothing to drink from.

Gerber pulled the top off the bottle, took a deep drink, and held it out. "Best I can do."

Karen took the bottle, drank deeply, and swallowed carefully, as if she was afraid that she had just set her throat on fire. Her eyes watered. She set the bottle on the floor and then sat on the bed. Slowly, she crossed her legs, letting her dress ride up above her knees. She leaned back on her elbows and stared at Gerber.

He moved to the bottle, capped it, and put it on the battered dresser. Then he turned to watch her.

Now she lifted her feet off the floor and hooked her heels on the rail of the cot. Her dress slid higher but apparently not far enough to suit her. She scratched her knee, pulling the material up until the tops of her stockings were visible. "You're not making this easy," she said.

"I'm sorry. I've been in the field for quite a while and it's nice just to be in the same room with a pretty woman."

"Thank you."

Gerber moved to the bed and reached for her hand. Instead of standing up, she pulled at him, tugging him down. He sat beside her as she turned to him. As they kissed, she pulled him down, so that they were side by side on the bed. For a minute they just kissed and then Gerber slid his hand along her thigh, reaching up under her dress until he felt the smooth side of her leg above her stocking. She sighed at his touch and pulled him closer.

He tried to draw back, and whispered, "Let me turn off the light."

"I don't mind." She held him tightly. "I don't mind at all."

Gerber moved to the left and Karen followed him so that

they both were fully on the bed. She rolled onto her back and hiked up her knees so that her skirt slid along her thighs, revealing her legs. Gerber touched her knee and let his hand slide up along her stocking until he was touching her bare skin. She rocked toward him, kissed him, and tried to unbutton his jungle jacket. While she did so, he attacked the buttons on her dress, reaching around her. When he got them all, he slipped it from her shoulders, leaned forward, and gently kissed them.

She got his jungle jacket off and tossed it to the floor. She sat there for a second, her dress bunched around her hips, and said, "Another awkward moment. How to get out of your clothes gracefully."

"I think if we help each other, we can do it." Gerber shrugged, taking off the shoulder holster that contained his .45 auto and that had been hidden under his jungle jacket. "Besides, how am I to gracefully get out of his holster. It just can't be done."

For a moment, she stared at the pistol as if it was something horrible. Horrible only because it reinforced where they were, who they were. In that moment, Karen realized that Gerber was involved in a deadly game, one that he had no control over. He wasn't just like the others she had met in Saigon, the ones who pretended to be warriors. He was a warrior, and the affection she was beginning to feel for him was underscored by the fact that he could be killed sometime soon. The thought scared her and for an instant she considered stopping everything so that she could get out. Then she lifted her arms so that he could pull her dress over her head. Instead of tossing it on the floor, Gerber stood up and folded it carefully. She sat up, swung around, and when he stepped back to the bed, she tried to unfasten his pants. That done, she pulled her slip up and took it off.

Gerber then turned off the light. An outside light flashed into the room in bursts so that movement seemed jerky like a series of still pictures. He watched Karen lean back and then roll to her side. She was wearing only her garter belt and stockings. He sat beside her and swung his feet up on the bed, pulling her close, enjoying the warmth of her smooth skin.

A few hours later she woke him gently, saying that she had to get to her room so that she wouldn't miss her transport back to Nha Trang.

Gerber threw back the sheet and said, "I'll walk you back."

"That's not necessary."

"I know. I want to."

Before he left her at the door of the building where the general housed all his guests, they exchanged addresses. He said that he would write and, if it was possible, would try to get to Nha Trang. He wanted to see her again, badly.

Five hours later he was on an army aviation Caribou, heading back to his camp. Crinshaw hadn't found him in the morning, but Bates had. And Bates gave him the bad news. During the night, while he was out drinking bourbon and chasing women, his base had been attacked. Bates didn't have many details, but he knew that it had been a heavy assault, and since he, Gerber, wasn't around, Bates had to order the air strikes.

But Bates wasn't particularly concerned. He said, "Don't worry. Crinshaw ordered you to Saigon. You had no choice. There is no worry there. And the assault proves that Charlie is in the area. You just keep documenting everything, just to cover your ass. Is there anything that I can do for you."

Gerber nodded and provided him with a written list. Bates glanced at it and nodded. "What's this soap powder."

"Soap flakes. Sully Smith wants it for one of his surprises."

"I don't think I can do anything about that. I think I can

have the rest of it for you. Got a Caribou scheduled to go out there with supplies. You can hop on that.''

Now, on the Caribou, just above the light mist that turned the whole countryside gray, Gerber couldn't help feeling strangely good. Part of it was getting back to his unit, although he had only been gone about twenty hours. But most of it was Karen.

He was sorry to have missed one of the biggest nights in camp. Charlie had arrived. In force. And he had been beaten. That felt good too.

CHAPTER 7 _____

First Lieutenant Jonathan Bromhead watched the UH-19 helicopter groan its way into the sky and chatter off toward Saigon, carrying Gerber to his meeting with the almighty Crinshaw, and silently prayed that Colonel Bates would be able to run interference for his commander. Bromhead had known Gerber for nearly a year and a half now, and liked the man intensely. He worried, however, about the captain's tendency to tell things exactly like they were. Bromhead believed that was the way you ought to do things, because accurate intelligence was important in waging successful combat; he'd learned that at West Point and relearned it over and over at Infantry Branch School, in Ranger School, and at the Special Warfare Center at Fort Bragg.

But in the little over two years he'd been on active duty in the U.S. Army, he'd also learned that generals—at least some of them, probably most of them, and certainly legs like Crinshaw—didn't always like you to do things the way they ought to be done. They liked you to do things the way they themselves wanted them done, and that meant not telling them things they didn't want to hear. Gerber was too good a soldier and too poor a politician to do that. The captain understood how the game was played, but he just couldn't force himself to play it. That kind of attitude could get you into big trouble with the brass hats, and Crinshaw was trouble enough already. When you're walking on eggs, it isn't smart to play hop-scotch.

Bromhead switched the heavy M-14 to his left hand and stuck out his right to the new guy. What was his name? All he could think of was Fettuccini and that wasn't right. The man's pack strap was covering his name tag, no help there.

"Jonathan Bromhead, the exec. You can call me Johnny, everybody else does. You're . . ." He left the question unfinished, hoping the man would help him out.

The new man gave him a funny look and said, "Master Sergeant Anthony B. Fetterman, Lieutenant. You can call me Master Sergeant. Everybody else does."

The snippy response startled Bromhead and he realized that the noncom had ignored his outstretched hand. Then he noticed that Fetterman had an old M-2 flamethrower in his right hand, and a heavy-looking duffel bag in the other. He felt his face turn hot and knew he was blushing, which made him even more embarrassed. Boy, this guy must really think I'm an idiot, he thought. He let the hand shift over toward the duffel bag.

"Here, let me give you a hand with your kit."

"Thanks, Lieutenant, but I can manage. If you'll just show me where I bunk."

"Right. Team bunker's this way. It's timber and sandbags right now. The concrete for the permanent one hasn't cured yet."

As they walked across the compound, Bromhead tried to figure out the new guy. There was something about him that just didn't seem right, besides the flamethrower. At first Bromhead thought it was the guy's size. He was a little fellow, both short and skinny. He looked like a good stiff breeze might bowl him over, yet he seemed to manage both the duffel bag and the flamethrower, each of which had to weigh close to seventy pounds, without difficulty. The guy had a dark complexion, Italian American maybe, or maybe Puerto Rican, although neither

seeemed to fit with the Fetterman name. Besides he didn't
have one of those mousy-looking mustaches the guys from
the Commonwealth all seemed so proud of.

Then it hit him. No facial hair at all. It was late afternoon,
and the guy's chin looked smooth as a baby's bottom.
Christ, thought Bromhead. This guy has spit-shined jungle
boots, pressed fatigues, and I'll bet he shaved on the way
out here in the ~~goddamn~~ helicopter. What the ~~hell~~ kind of
garret trooper have they saddled us with? Then he noticed
the eyes. Not blue, not brown. Blueblack and cold like
steel. It made him feel creepy, looking at those eyes, and
he looked away across the compound, at the construction,
at the wire, anywhere but at those eyes.

There was nobody in the team bunker when they got
there and Bromhead showed Fetterman to an area screened
off with tarpaulins.

"This was Schattschneider's bunk. The guy you're
replacing," Bromhead said. "I guess you can have it, if
you don't mind."

"Why should I mind, Lieutenant? He's dead, ain't he?
He sure as ~~hell~~ ain't going to mind. If he don't, why
should I?"

Fetterman set the flamethrower and the duffel against
the sandbagged wall of the bunker, shrugged his way out
of the field pack, and took off his jungle jacket, revealing
a large-framed revolver in a shoulder holster under his
right armpit, with an unidentifiable combat knife in a
sheath taped to the outside of the holster. Bromhead thought
the pistol might be a .44 magnum Smith and Wesson, but
he'd never seen one with such a short barrel.

Fetterman took his bedroll, a poncho and blanket liner,
and unrolled it on the cot. The entire surface of the blanket
was covered with little snapped straps, holding every kind
of dagger, throwing knife, shuriken, and machete imaginable. There was a bundle of short arrows with razor-sharp,
broad-head points that Bromhead recognized as crossbow
bolts, and a dozen tiny darts with their points covered by

something that looked like cosmoline, the tips protected by little corks.

Good God, thought Bromhead. This guy's come to Vietnam prepared to fight the Crusades all over again. He reached for one of the darts. "What are these—"

"Don't touch those."

"Take it easy, Sergeant, I was just curious about—"

"I said keep your ~~fucking~~ hands off those darts."

Fetterman seized his wrist suddenly. There was surprising strength in the man's grip for such a little person. Bromhead realized he couldn't have moved his hand if he'd wanted to.

"Sir," said the sergeant more calmly, "I must respectfully inform you that those darts are coated with curare, a fast-acting poison that affects the central nervous system. If you insist on examining them, you should be aware that should even a slight amount of the poison enter your body, you will be paralyzed within a matter of seconds and dead long before the team medic could get here and determine that there is nothing he can do for you anyway. Now then, sir, if you would still like to examine them, go ahead. Be my guest."

He released his grip, and Bromhead carefully rubbed his wrist. He had no doubt that a bruise would develop by morning.

"Ah, no thanks, Sergeant. I'm really not that interested in darts. But as long as we're on the subject, I believe that it's my duty to inform you that the folks in Geneva who are in the business of writing up rules about such things take a dim view of using poisonous projectiles."

"Would they be the same folks who drew up the rules that say you can't use poisonous, asphyxiating, or other gases, including tear gas, back in 1925, Lieutenant? You know, the Geneva protocol on gas warfare that the good old U.S. of A. Senate Foreign Relations Committee refused to ratify? Those same folks who think dumdum bullets are too inhumane to be used in warfare, but okay for police officers to use against civilians? Those same folks who think napalm and white phosphorus are just fine for killing people in a nice, humane, and legal manner?''

Bromhead shrugged. "I didn't say the rules made sense."

"Neither did Charlie, Lieutenant, and we both know what he dips his pungi stakes in."

Fetterman took off his paratrooper helmet and removed the padlock from his duffel bag. He took out a second poncho, spread it out next to his bunk, and dumped the contents of the bag out on it. The only items of clothing were some socks, another pair of jungle boots, a pair of jump boots, and two sets of tiger-striped fatigues with about fifty pockets sewn all over them. The rest of the pile was a collection of ammunition, magazines, grenades, flares, three or four weapons that had been broken down into parts so they would fit in the duffel, and one or two objects Bromhead couldn't begin to identify.

Bromhead considered saying something to Fetterman about wearing his shoulder holster concealed beneath his jungle jacket, a violation of both military regulations and the laws of land warfare established at Geneva, but then figured, why bother? If I tell this guy to stop using a shoulder holster under his clothes, he'll probably just put the damned thing in his pocket. He's been in the army a long time, he's developed his own way of doing things that work for him, and he sure as hell isn't going to be changed overnight by some college boy first looie with three whole days of combat experience under his belt. I just hope he and I can learn to work together pretty quickly, because if we can't, then we're both going to have a lot of problems.

Instead he said, "I've got a few things to check on. Why don't you get your stuff squared away and then come find me and I'll introduce you to the rest of the team and our Vietnamese counterparts. After that we'll find you some chow and decide where to put you tonight. Captain Gerber has standing orders for full alert for the team and our company of Tai strikers after midnight. The Vietnamese will only do fifty percent. Do I need to ask if you can handle an eighty-one or a fifty?''

''No, Lieutenant, you don't need to ask if I can handle an eighty-one or a fifty. But there is something you need to ask.''

''What's that?''

''I don't speak Vietnamese or Tai.''

Bromhead looked at the man incredulously.

''Saigon said you were fluent in half a dozen languages.''

''I am,'' said Fetterman, calmly fitting a two-piece blow gun together and leaning it next to the flamethrower. ''I speak English, German, Russian, Spanish, Lowland Lao, Hmong, and a little French. I'm also quite good with Arabic. I just don't happen to know any Tai or Vietnamese.''

''Well, ████ me, over,'' said Bromhead.

Fetterman gave him a big grin. ''████ you, Lieutenant, out.''

For various reasons, the evening meal wasn't until after dark. The entire camp had stood to at dusk, and the LPs had gone out immediately afterward, composed this time of two all-Tai teams, one under the bloodthirsty Sergeant Krung, the other led by a corporal handpicked by Lieutenant Bao. The third LP was made up of Vietnamese Regional Forces commanded by Special Forces Sergeant Luong and advised by Sergeant Cavanaugh. Apparently Captain Trang had overheard a chance remark by Luong that the LLDB commander had interpreted as casting doubt on his abilities to engage the enemy. As punishment for so rude an insult, Trang had ordered Luong to take four men from the RFs and lead one of the LP teams. This had created no great distress with Luong, who understood the necessity of the LPs, even if he wasn't totally enthusiastic about the duty. Who was? Sergeant Cavanaugh was delighted with the arrangement as he had already developed a close working relationship with Luong, since both men were communication specialists, and he had found the LLDB sergeant to be both likable and reliable. Cavanaugh and Luong took their team out to a position near the bridge northwest of the camp, scene of the brief but sharp fight between Tyme's team and the Viet Cong rocket and machine gun teams two nights before. Following standard procedures, they did not reoccupy the site of the previous LP, but moved off a few dozen meters to one side before digging in and setting up their .30-caliber machine gun and BAR. All the LPs had beefed up their armament a bit because of the previous attack.

Back in camp, those Green Berets not already standing a watch settled down to a supper of rice, bamboo shoots, peppers, and fish chunks, washed down with tepid tea from the valiantly struggling refrigerator. Bromhead introduced Fetterman to those team members the master sergeant had not already met, and each welcomed him to the team with all the enthusiastic reserve that befitted a new man coming on board.

About halfway through the meal, Charlie sent his own welcome in the form of three incoming mortar rounds. They hit well outside the inner perimeter, and did no particular damage. The Viet Cong repeated the pattern every couple of hours throughout the night. The VC mortar crew would fire off a few rounds, then hump their mortar somewhere else before Kittredge, up in the FCT, could vector any effective return fire on them. The Cong would then wait until things settled down good in camp, and let off another three rounds, then head out of there to someplace else. It wasn't serious shooting. They were just trying to keep everybody in the camp awake, unaware that most of them would be awake after midnight anyway.

After supper, Master Sergeant Fetterman and Sergeant First Class Tyme took out a ten-man roving ambush patrol, made up of eight Tais. All the soldiers were wearing tiger-striped fatigues, and were heavily armed. The patrol carried two PRC-10 radios and two PRC-6s for communications. Weapons consisted of two BARs, two M-79 grenade launchers, M-3 submachine guns, and M-2 carbines. Tyme had his ever-present shotgun, and Fetterman carried an older model M-3 equipped with a silencer, one of a thousand or so that had been developed for use by the OSS toward the end of World War II. He was wearing his custom-tailored no-see-me's and the pockets were crammed full of magazines, grenades, and flares, which were to be used both for signaling and for illuminating the killing zone should a suitable target be found to spring an ambush on. He was also wearing a flak vest under his jungle jacket, and his helmet, and immediately received a good-natured jibe from Tyme about his "dome protector."

"Son, how much combat time you got?" Fetterman asked.

Tyme admitted that it was less than a week.

"Uh-huh. Yeah," replied Fetterman. "I was in France and Germany during Two. I was in Korea. I've been up against the Pathet Lao in Laos, and I was in Cuba during the Bay of Pigs fiasco. Every war I've been in, I've been shelled, mortared, and grenaded, sometimes during a night ambush just like this one. Me and this funny steel pot, we're inseparable. I don't intend to go home to Mrs. Fetterman and the kids in some box just because people made fun of my hat. You'll notice I painted it green for you, though."

After the patrol moved out, Bromhead walked the walls, checking that each man was alert at his post and that all the crew-served weapons in the bunkers were manned and ready. After that, it was just a question of wait and see.

A little after ten o'clock Charlie sent a few mortar rounds in the general direction of the camp, and a few more after midnight. Then, nothing happened until half-past one, when Bromhead got a radio call from Fetterman, saying that Charlie seemed to be running a number of small patrols a couple of klicks out from the camp, indicating that something definitely was up. As such, Fetterman intended to hold off on the ambush and see what developed. It was, he felt, just possible that a larger target might present itself.

About forty minutes later, Sergeant Cavanaugh, manning LP-1 near the bridge with Luong and four RFs, reported that he could hear splashing upstream from the bridge. His call was followed almost immediately by a report from LP-2 near the bend in the river southwest of the camp that there was a great deal of movement going on southeast of their position, apparently on the near side of the river. Remembering Sergeant Krung's tendency to be tight-lipped, Bromhead immediately called him on the radio. This evening, however, the Tai noncom answered immediately, but informed him that he had seen or heard no sign of enemy movement, as yet. Bromhead told him to report at once if he did, and then climbed up into the fire control tower with Kittredge and Duong; they were joined shortly by Lieutenant Minh. Both Kittredge and Bromhead studied the terrain outside the camp carefully through infrared scopes, but neither could detect any movement. Then, just as he was about to lower his scope, Bromhead took one last look directly west of the camp, toward the river.

"Oh Jesus Christ!" he said. "Would you look at those bastards come."

A reinforced company of black-pajama-clad Viet Cong were running through the high elephant grass straight toward the west wall.

"Steve," said Bromhead, "bearing two-seven zero. Get some willy pete on those mothers. Now!" He was already reaching for the two telephones that connected with the 81mm mortar pits.

Holding a telephone handset to either side of his head, Bromhead called for illumination west of camp. As the first outgoing rounds whumped out of the tubes, Bromhead heard a loud, shuddering whir, followed immediately by a sharp, metallic clang as the camp began to take incoming mortar fire.

While Bromhead was talking to the mortar crews in the eighty-one pits and Kittredge was getting a range and bearing estimate on the VC troops, Sergeant Duong was ringing up the 60mm mortar pits. Lieutenant Minh sent a runner to rouse the rest of the RF strikers and fetch Captain Trang, then he called Staff Sergeant Bocker in the commo bunker. Minh asked to speak with Staff Sergeant Lim, Bocker's counterpart, but was told that he was not there. Minh, secretly relieved that he would not have to deal with his own air force, then asked Bocker to put in a request for the nearest available American flare ship.

For little over a minute the VC mortars pounded the camp with high-explosive shells, while Kittredge, working closely with Duong, did his best to lay white phosphorus eggs smack in the laps of the advancing VC infantry. It quickly became apparent, however, that at least some of the VC mortars were concentrating on clearing a path through the barbed wire and mines surrounding the camp. As soon as he noted this, Bromhead directed Kittredge to divert two of the sixties to return fire on the enemy mortars. Due to the height of the fire control tower and the absence of any significant intervening slopes surrounding the camp, Kittredge was able to get a fix on several VC mortar positions.

Suddenly there was a new addition to the cacophony of battle. An eerie trilling filled the air: the sound of bugles.

Within seconds, the entire west wall opened fire. The range was still too great for carbines and submachine guns, and the poor light was not conducive to well-aimed rifle fire, but the .50- and .30-caliber machine guns were doing a job on the front ranks of the VC assault force. The recoilless rifles and bazookas crewed by the Tais blasted holes in the rear ranks with high-explosive and white phosphorus rounds, and the mortars kept up their deadly rain of fire and steel. The VC were up to the outer wire now, and the crews on the sixties were dropping charge-three rounds down the tubes at the rate of one every four seconds.

As the VC reached the wire and the smaller weapons began to have some effect along with the machine guns, the communist advance seemed to hesitate. It was only then that Bromhead became aware of the steadily ringing telephone in front of him. It was the line connecting to LP-3. With a sickening feeling growing in the pit of his stomach, Bromhead snatched the handset to his ear and shouted "Go ahead!" Then he listened for a moment and shouted again.

Whirling about, he grabbed up an IR scope and scanned the area to the southeast of the camp. The sick feeling in his stomach solidified to lead as he stared, not wanting to believe, at what had to be nearly a battalion of Viet Cong. "I knew it! I knew it! Those bastards are going to hit us on both walls at once!"

Furiously, he pounded Kittredge on the shoulder to get his attention, then pointed and shouted in the heavy-weapons specialist's ear to make himself heard over the din of firing.

"Swing number-one and number-two sixty around and give them four rounds of WP and then four HE, charge three. Then go to charge two and keep it up. We're about to get hit with a ton of shit!"

"Where the hell is that flare ship?"

Bromhead turned to his Vietnamese counterpart. "Lieutenant Minh, round up a squad—"

"I'll need more than a squad if I'm going out there, old boy," quipped Minh.

"And reinforce the eastern part of the south wall," Bromhead continued. "We're about to be in deep trouble. Take a couple of BAR teams with you."

"Oh, it's still a holding action, is it?" Minh nodded his understanding and let drop the telephone he'd been using to report on the battle to Captain Trang, who was now safely ensconced in the command bunker beneath the FCT.

Bromhead didn't wait to watch him go. He was already cranking up number-one eighty-one pit to get some illumination southeast of the camp.

"Sweet mother of God," he whispered. "Where in the hell is that flare ship?"

CHAPTER 8

On the ambush patrol, Master Sergeant Fetterman suddenly found himself with far more targets than ambushers.

Recognizing the danger of attacking so numerically large a force of enemy, which appeared to be on all sides of his position, he pulled the ambush team into a tight defensive circle and ordered his men to hold their fire and let the VC pass. Recalling from his study of maps earlier in the day that a fairly large clearing was nearby, and noting that most of the Viet Cong passing by his position had gone in that direction before apparently moving on toward the camp, Fetterman discussed the possibility with Tyme that the VC might be planning to use the clearing as an initial rallying point after the attack on the Green Beret camp. Tyme agreed that the idea seemed plausible, and the two men decided to shift the ambush to cover the clearing, thereby catching, they hoped, some of the returning communists. They radioed Bromhead that they were changing their location, giving approximate range and bearing from their original ambush site. This let Bromhead know not to train mortar fire on the suspected VC rally point, without giving away where they were moving to, should any English-speaking VC be monitoring their radio frequency. Several possible ambush sites had been discussed that afternoon by Tyme, Fetterman, and Bromhead, and identified by alphanumerics as a means of thwarting enemy communications intelligence. The Americans had had no way of knowing if the local VC forces were sophisticated enough to be able to monitor their radio traffic, and had not taken any chances.

Upon approaching the clearing, Fetterman once again deployed the men in the defensive circle; then he and Tyme crawled cautiously forward to check out the clearing. Taking an image metascope from one of the many pockets on his tiger-striped fatigues, Fetterman carefully studied the clearing, noting two VC armed with SKS carbines who had been left behind to guard the clearing. Without comment, he handed the small infrared light source and viewing device to Tyme, who also studied the clearing, then tapped Fetterman's hand twice, indicating he had also seen the two guards. Although the two Americans were lying next to each other, it was too dark for them to see one another without the aid of the image metascope.

Satisfied that Tyme had seen the same number of guards as he had, Fetterman silently slipped out his Case VS-21 combat knife, then touched Tyme's hand to it to indicate his intention. Tyme drew his own knife, a Marine Corps issue Kabar, and repeated Fetterman's gesture, indicating he understood. Checking the position of the guards a final time with the night viewing device, the two men crawled quietly toward their respective targets.

Fetterman dispatched his man in textbook fashion. As he crawled up to the man, illumination rounds from the camp's 81mm mortar began popping east of the clearing. The sickly yellow-green glare from the parachute flares was sufficiently far from the clearing to not really illuminate it, but the residual light was enough to show the outline of the guard. It also momentarily distracted the attention of both VC. Fetterman calmly rose up off the ground and, moving with catlike agility despite his heavily loaded jungle jacket, clapped a hand over the guard's nose and mouth, and drove the blade of the Case fighting knife up through the man's kidney and into his left lung, then pulled the man backward and slashed the knife across his throat, severing the larnyx from the trachea and cutting through both carotid arteries.

Tyme was not quite so professional in dispatching his man. The simple truth of the matter was that he had never killed a man with a knife before. Indeed, except for the brief, intense fight the first night, when the base had been rocketed and mortared and the VC had tried to probe the wire, Tyme had never killed anyone. He had not been particularly upset by that initial encounter with death. He knew from a dozen World War II movies and countless episodes of "Combat!" that the new guy was supposed to go off somewhere and puke after making his first kill, but he hadn't felt ill at all, just amazed. He clearly remembered thinking, Jeez, these guys are really ~~fucked~~ up, when he looked at the bodies afterward. Did we do all that? Did I do that? Man! We really ~~fucked~~ these guys up.

But there is a great deal of difference between killing an enemy with a grenade or a shotgun in a firefight and sneaking up behind a man in the dark and killing him with a knife. It's a more personal kind of death, a more deliberate killing. Just as he stepped up to the man, the VC guard either heard or sensed Tyme's presence and turned, staring him straight in the face. To his credit, Tyme did not hesitate. He twisted his wrist to bring the combat Bowie blade up, drove it in up to the hilt just above the man's web belt, and ripped upward until he hit ribs. The man grunted as he fell, then started to cry out something in Vietnamese. Tyme brought his boot down on the man's neck, snapping it, and cutting the cry off short.

Momentarily, Tyme became aware that he was still grinding his foot on the VC's neck. His knife, hand, and the sleeve of his tiger-striped jungle jacket were covered with blood. In the flickering light of the distant flares, he could see Fetterman standing next to him.

"You all right, kid?" the master sergeant asked.

"I'm okay." Tyme nodded. "It's his blood."

"I meant the leg," said Fetterman, not meaning the leg at all. "Your leg is bleeding."

Tyme looked down. His left thigh was bleeding. He examined it, but it appeared to be only a shallow cut. "Well, I'll be a ring-tailed son of a bitch. How'd that happen?"

"Looks like you were a little slow," said Fetterman, indicating the bayonet on the VC's carbine. "He drew blood too."

"Yeah, well, he didn't draw enough. Stupid bastard should have shot me." He kicked the body, then stooped and wiped his knife on the dead guard's shirt before sheathing it.

"Come on," said Fetterman. "Let's get these bodies out of here and get the ambush set up. Then we better get something on that leg of yours before it decides to get infected."

Tyme looked down disgustedly at the cut on his leg, then flashed Fetterman a grin. "Best argument I know of for using a silencer."

Fetterman hefted his submachine gun. "I thought of that, but this thing's kind of noisy even with a silencer. Besides, you had a shotgun. I'd have had to shoot both of them, and I couldn't be sure of getting a good hit on the second. Light's too poor. I might have missed, or only wounded him, and then we'd have had all kinds of trouble."

"I didn't mean that as a criticism," said Tyme.

"And I didn't mean that as an apology. Let's get moving."

In the fire control tower, Bromhead had abandoned the infrared scope. With flares popping west and southeast of the camp, the device was nearly useless, as the glare of the illumination rounds kept washing out the image in the scope. If anything happened north of the camp, the people on the north wall would have to deal with it, as would those on the east wall. Bromhead didn't consider attack from either of those directions likely now, since he had sizable enemy forces converging on his position from the west and southeast, and any VC attacking from the north or east would run the risk of taking fire from the Cong already hitting the defenders. Charlie was still dropping mortar rounds all over the airstrip, and somewhere out near the river, a couple of twelve-sevens had opened up, their green and white tracers tearing ragged holes in the air over the base. The bullets from the heavy machine guns weren't doing much damage, however, as they were arcing high over the camp, apparently trying to knock out the fire control tower.

Trip flares were going up all over the place as the VC broke through the outer perimeter, either running through gaps the mortars had knocked in the wire or simply flopping down on the coils of concertina, so that the men behind them could leap over their bodies and rush the walls. Kittredge was talking as fast as he could to the mortar pits on the field telephones, while Sergeant Duong took the range and bearing readings. Except for the eighty-ones firing flares and the two sixties designated to occupy the VC mortars, every mortar crew was chucking out HE at charge two as as fast as they could pull the increments and drop the rounds down the tubes.

Along the west and south walls, everyone was putting out rounds, and the southern third of the east wall had joined in, firing at the VC attacking from the southeast. There was some sporadic firing on the south side of the camp, but they were all shooting at shadows, just firing out of fear, without any real targets.

Fifties were pounding, every fifth round a tracer, floating out from the camp like great red baseballs. The thirties were hammering away, and the deep-throated chug-chug of BARs mixed with the rattle of carbines and submachine guns. VC were hitting trip wires between the perimeters east of the camp and grenades and mines were going off.

Bromhead grabbed Kittredge's shoulder. "Steve, screw

those mortars. We've got to get some more on that bunch southeast. There's got to be three times as many of them, and four sixties just aren't going to do it.''

Kittredge nodded and grabbed up another field phone. With Duong's assitance, he redirected the two mortars that had been lobbing white phosphorus rounds at the enemy mortar positions to fire high-explosive rounds on the VC battalion attacking the camp's southern defenses.

As the mortars shifted away from the Viet Cong company attacking from the west, the VC surged forward despite the mines, boobytrapped grenades, and the withering fire from the bunkers and men on the wall. Bromhead grabbed the special direct line to the command bunker and cranked the handle furiously. He was answered immediately.

''Smith. Go ahead.''

''Sully, they're almost up to the inner wire. Now's the time. Do the west wall, Repeat, west wall.''

''It'll be a pleasure, sir.''

In the command bunker, while Trang, Hinh, and Lim— the LLDB Commo Sergeant who should have been in the communications bunker with Bocker— huddled nervously in the corner, covering the doorway with their tommy guns, Staff Sergeant Smith got calmly up from his folding steel chair, took two paces across the bunker, and pulled aside a sandbag, revealing a small wooden panel holding several switches. With two fingers from each hand, he calmly flipped the four switches labeled WEST 1-2-3-4.

Just outside the inner defensive ring of barbed wire stretching along the entire west wall and fifteen meters in front of the moat, the ground erupted in a shattering explosion. Sixteen claymore mines and several hundred yards of PETN-filled detonator cord had instantly blown up when Smith closed the four switches, sending thousands upon thousands of steel balls out in a series of ever-widening fans that cut men off at the knees, cut heads off at the neck, cut too-close bodies in half, and delivered a fatal case of the measles over a fifty-meter-wide area, fifty meters out in front of each mine, maiming and wounding as far as a hundred and fifty or two hundred meters.

The force of Viet Cong soldiers attacking the west side of the camp suddenly ceased to be a serious problem, although the men on the wall kept firing for several minutes, shooting whenever a wounded enemy or a shadow moved or was imagined to move.

In the command bunker, Smith stepped back and picked up the dangling telephone handset again. "How was that, sir?" he asked.

"Incredible," Bromhead told him. "Just fucking unbelievable. Hang on the line, Sully. We're going to have to blow the south wall pretty quickly."

"Right, Lieutenant," said Smith. "I'll be right here holding the phone. Just holler when you want it."

Lieutenant Minh, meanwhile, had somewhat loosely interpreted Bromhead's advice to get together a squad with a couple of BARs and reinforce the south wall. Minh had always been the sort of soldier who interpreted orders somewhat loosely, but also got the job done. In this instance, he interpreted a squad to be something less than a platoon, and a couple of BARs to be anything less than half a dozen. By pulling a few men off the north wall and the northern part of the west wall, grabbing Sergeant Tam, the Vietnamese assistant medical specialist who wasn't yet needed in the infirmary, and Sergeants Vo and Suong, the two demolitions experts who had been commanding bunker positions on the north wall, and finally threatening to shoot a few RFs hiding behind sandbags if they didn't get up and fight, he managed to scrape up about twenty men, including four BAR teams. And since no one had said he shouldn't do so, he took a .30-caliber light machine gun team and a couple of M-79 grenade launchers as well.

The two dozen men arrived at the southeast corner of the camp just as the first company of the VC battalion attacking from south breached the outer wire, and the sudden addition of five automatic weapons, two grenade launchers, and a dozen and a half M-2 carbines and submachine guns to the already formidable defense, stopped the enemy advance cold. The VC company faltered, started to fall back, then were pushed forward again by the second company coming up behind them.

All six of the camp's 60mm mortars were now shelling the area south of the camp at charge one.

The flare ship, a U.S. Air Force C-47, had finally arrived and begun to drop large aerial flares, which brilliantly lit the entire area south and west of the camp and freed the two 81mm mortars from the necessity of firing illumination rounds. The 81s now began pounding the third company of VC coming up to the outer wire with high-explosive shells. Still the communist guerrillas came forward.

In the fire control tower, Bromhead shouted into the telephone, "Now, Sully! Now!"

In the command bunker, Sergeant Smith closed three switches controlling the claymore mines covering the south wall, releasing a torrent of hot steel death. The Viet Cong advance once again faltered.

East of the camp, Fetterman's ambush party had deployed along the east edge of the clearing, with minimal flank security, to await the arrival of the VC who were falling back to their rallying point. Fetterman had sited the four claymore mines he and Tyme had carried along either side of the clearing, two to north, two to south.

As the shattered, wounded, and frightened VC began to drift in, there was clearly some consternation caused by the absense of the two sentries who had been eliminated earlier, but as Fetterman did not speak Vietnamese, he was unable to follow exactly what was said. When it appeared that about two dozen men had entered the clearing, Fetterman blew a sharp blast on his whistle and began firing.

As Tyme and the rest of the ambush party opened up, the Viet Cong were thrown into complete confusion, rushing in all directions. Fetterman waited as long as possible, then touched off the claymores. About a dozen VC were knocked down like bowling pins.

Several of the panic-stricken VC rushed straight toward the ambushers. Fetterman looked up from the claymore firing switches to see one man almost on top of him and realized his M-3 had an empty magazine in it. Fetterman knew the first rule of combat shooting was to change magazines immediately, but he had ignored that rule in order to detonate the claymore. Now there was no time for self-recrimination. As the man continued forward, Fetterman rose off the ground less than two feet in front of him and clubbed the VC soldier in the throat with his submachine gun. As the man went down, Fetterman drew the .44 magnum revolver from under his jungle jacket, popping off a button in the process, and shot the man once in the face.

Fetterman quickly dropped back into the grass, rolled a short distance to one side, and changed the magazines in the submachine gun before sticking his head back up. He squeezed off three long bursts, followed them with a grenade pitched far out into the clearing, then changed magazines again as the grenade went off.

A small group of VC had gotten organized in the trees at the far side of the clearing and were putting up a fairly heavy volume of return fire, working methodically with fire and maneuver, trying to flank the ambush. Fetterman yelled to Tyme to take three men and out flank the flankers, then grabbed an M-79 from the Tai grenadier next to him and put a round on top of the VC fire team providing cover for the maneuver element. As he stuck out his hand, the grenadier alertly slapped another round into it, and Fetterman, working quickly, put three more of the 40mm grenades into the treeline. The enemy firing slackened but did not stop.

Whoever those little mothers are, thought Fetterman, they are one little bunch of tough nuts. I wonder how come they fight so much better than the rest of these clowns?

Suddenly the ambushers started taking automatic weapons fire from the left flank as the VC maneuver team got into position and began shooting up the Tais. Fetterman's devastatingly successful ambush suddenly seemed on the verge of being routed.

Then the grenades went off, followed immediately by the sharp rattle of automatic carbines and the thunderous boom-boom, boom-boom, boom-boom, of Tyme's shotgun, and it was all over. The VC flankers were dead, and the firing from across the clearing trickled away and died as the VC slipped off into the woods.

Fetterman shouted, "Cease fire! Cease fire!" since he didn,t know any Tai, and then yelled *"Cessez tirant! Cessez tirant!"* Slowly, the Tais stopped shooting.

Tyme passed slowly out of the trees and into the edge of the clearing, accompanied by his three Tais, one of whom had been wounded in the arm. The light-weapons specialist had his Browning pistol in his right hand, the shotgun resting in the crook of his right elbow while he stuffed shells into the magazine with his left hand.

Fetterman looked up and smiled at the young sergeant. "Well, well," he said. "If it isn't Boom-Boom Tyme and his Remington hand-howitzer. Nice work, Boom-Boom."

The other man gave him a pained look. "Justin Tyme, if you please."

"But of course you were, my boy. Of course you were. Come on, Boom-Boom, let's police up the weapons and documents and get the ~~hell~~ out of here."

Heavy fighting was still raging all along the southern wall of the camp. In the bunkers, men were pouring water from their canteens on the barrels of machine guns, trying futilely to keep the weapons cool enough to keep working.

The .50-caliber in the key southwest corner bunker had already seized tight. The center of the camp was still taking incoming mortar rounds, and the situation did not look good.

Still, Bromhead, who had remained in the fire control tower with Kittredge and Duong where he had better visibility to direct the fighting, had almost begun to believe that they might be able to hold the camp. There had already been some hand-to-hand fighting on the wall, but the VC had been pushed back once more. Then, out of the distance, Bromhead saw a long line of back-pajama-clad men advancing some distance behind the third VC company. The communist commander had committed his reserves. There must have been two hundred men.

Bromhead called Smith in the command bunker and told him to strip the north wall defenses. "Sully, take every third man off the north wall. Pull one of the thirties off the north and another off the east, and take those two three-five teams off the east wall with you. Get another BAR from somewhere, and get down to the south wall and reinforce Minh."

"Yes sir."

"And Sully . . ."

"Yes sir?"

"Keep that thick head of yours down, okay?"

"Yes sir."

Realizing they were about to be reinforced, the third VC company, along with the remains of the first two companies, surged forward, firing, yelling, hurling grenades and satchel charges. Many succeeded in throwing ladders and planks across the pungi-stake-filled moat and clawing their way up the earthen embankment.

The fighting once more turned into hand-to-hand combat. Carbines were swung like baseball bats. Tais and RFs with bayonets fixed to heavy Garand rifles clashed atop the wall with Viet Cong soldiers with spiked bayoneted SKSs and old French MAS rifles nearly as heavy as the Garands.

Knives and machetes flashed under the harsh glare of flares, and grenades exploded on both sides of the wall, filling the air with shrapnel. Cries of "Medic!" and *"Bac Se!"* mingled with the screams of the wounded and the moans of the dying, and through it all, the machine guns kept hammering, hammering, hammering, until the bolts seized or the barrels melted down. In the southeast corner bunker, the barrel of the only remaining .50-caliber machine gun capable of being brought to bear on the Viet Cong had become so hot that it had turned plastic, swiveling around of its own accord like a garden hose held too far back from the nozzel, spraying tracers all over the place like crazy Roman candles.

In the fire control tower, Bromhead watched with macabre fascination as Smith arrived with the reinforcements, and the men had to fight their way through a small knot of VC who had somehow gotten over the wall and into the camp before they could set up their machine guns and BARs.

"Hold them. Hold them," Bromhead whispered to himself, then resignedly picked up his M-14 and began sniping at the occasional VC soldier attempting to climb over the wall. He shot three before Kittredge touched his arm and motioned toward the PRC-10.

"TAC Air on the radio," he said by way of explanation.

Bromhead pressed the handset against his ear and heard, "Zulu Six, Zulu Six. This is Puff, over."

"Puff, this is Zulu Five. Six is unavailable, over."

"Ah, roger, Five. Crystal Ball thought perhaps you boys might need some assistance, so old Puff is here with forty thousand rounds of joy. Where do you want it, over."

It took Bromhead a second to realize what the pilot meant. Crystal Ball was B-team headquarters in Saigon. Bocker, in the commo bunker, would, of course, have been in constant contact with B-team, keeping them apprised of the situation. It had not been really apparent to

Bromhead that he would need air support until it had been to late to call for it. Evidently someone at B-team, Bates, or possibly even Gerber if he were there, had recognized the danger and set the wheels in motion before things had actually degenerated that far.

"Joy, Puff," said Bromhead. "Put it immediately south of the camp. The enemy is on the southern perimeter."

"Understand south side of camp, Zulu Five."

"Negative. Negative. Southern perimeter. Do not, repeat, do not, fire on the south wall of the camp. Put it between the wires. Don't put it on the camp. We've got the camp, those people don't have it. We have friendlies on the south wall. Put it south of the camp. Over."

"Roger. Understand south of the camp, between the wires."

"That's affirmative. Do you require that we mark with fire arrow?"

"Not necessary, Zulu Five. That's where all the fighting is, right?"

"Right."

"Coming right down. Puff out."

The pilot of the AC-47 Dragon gunship, brought the World War II vintage converted transport down in a tight turn and flew parallel to the southern wall of the camp. As he came up even with the camp, the twin-engine plane in a steep left bank, he touched the firing button and three General Electric mini-guns in the cargo compartment gave a long burp. With each gun firing six thousand rounds per minute, the 7.62mm tracers, one every fifth round, seemed to make three unbroken lines to the ground, like some fancy neon sign.

The Dragon ship pilot made two more passes, chopping up the three Viet Cong companies between the barbed-wire perimeters, and cutting down the two-hundred-man reserve company like a hay mower. The VC attack on Special Forces Camp A-555 was over.

"Puff. Puff. This is Zulu Five," said Bromhead. "Many thanks for the assist. I think we can handle it now. Over."

"Rog. Zulu Five. Glad to help. Call us anytime. Puff out."

The camp continued to take some desultory mortar fire throughout the remainder of the night, but it was simple harassing fire, and there were no further casualties. Lieutenant Minh had been cut on the chin and hand during the hand-to-hand fighting on the south wall, but was not seriously injured. The defenders of Special Forces Camp A-555 had suffered fifteen Tai and RF strikers dead and thirty-seven wounded. Sully Smith had had a tooth knocked out by a VC rifle butt. There were no other casualties among the Americans in the camp.

Toward dawn, even the harassing fire from the VC mortars ceased and Bromhead and Minh organized work parties to clean up the camp, repair defenses, and fill in the holes in the runway. A major supply shipment was due in at ten by U.S. Army Aviation Caribou. Captain Trang did not prove to be any great assistance during the cleanup operations, but neither did he prove to be much of a hindrance, being "occupied with official duties," in his private quarters. Shortly after 0700 a Chinook helicopter came in from Bien Hoa and medivaced the wounded. A couple of South Vietnamese Air Force UH-19s came in about an hour later and flew out the bodies of the dead.

In the general hubbub and confusion, Bromhead had more or less forgotten about the LPs until the Tais came straggling in. Sergeant Krung looked particularly dejected because despite all the fighting last night, he had not personally been in a position to kill a single Viet Cong.

When Fetterman and Tyme came back in with the ambush patrol, Bromhead took them aside and informed them that Cavanaugh and Luong's LP had not returned and, worse, could not be reached either by radio or the field telephone. Bromhead feared the worst.

"I know you guys just got in and you're beat, but if you and Minh can keep things running long enough, I'd like to take a—"

"Forget it, Lieutenant," said Fetterman. "You take a patrol out to collect them and leave the camp with no American officers? That wouldn't do at all if Big Green decided to drop in on us. Boom-Boom here and I'll get together a couple of men and go out and have a look-see."

"Boom-Boom?" queried Bromhead.

"Never mind," said Tyme sourly. "I'm sure Master Sergeant Fetterman will explain later. Probably at great length. He seems to think it's v-e-r-y f-u-n-n-y."

"Okay, later then. Take Doc McMillan with you, or Washington if the doc's too busy."

They found Sean Cavanaugh sitting on the earthen embankment of the large foxhole that had been LP-1. He just sat there motionless as they walked up. His eyes were red and dry, but his cheeks were soaked with tears. His uniform was crusted with dried blood, only a little of which was his own. He was slack-shouldered, and had the broken-off stock of a carbine in one hand and an entrenching tool in the other. Both had blood on them.

Sergeant Luong and the four RFs were dead. They had been dead for several hours. There was not one single round of ammunition in any of their weapons or ammo belts. Both the radio and the field phone had been shot full of holes. Two of the RFs had died with knives in or near their hands. Luong had died with his fingers clenched about the throat of a Viet Cong soldier who had driven the spike bayonet of an SKS clear through the young Vietnamese commo sergeant's body, entering just under the left armpit and exiting between the lower right ribs. The Viet Cong soldier was even younger than Luong.

Tyme stood still, taking it all in and not wanting to believe it. In the foxhole, on top of the RFs, in a large

ragged circle surrounding the LP, were bodies and more
bodies and more bodies. At least a full platoon of Viet
Cong dead.

Fetterman walked forward and carefully disarmed Cavanaugh. There was a single large tear rolling slowly down
the master sergeant's cheek as he put his arm gently
around Cavanaugh's shoulders and helped him to his
feet.

"Come on, son," said Fetterman. "You made it. You're
alive. Let's go back into camp now."

The patrol walked back to camp without anyone saying
another word.

CHAPTER 9 _____

The rest of the morning passed pretty much uneventfully. Instead of the expected Caribou, the routine supply helicopter arrived about ten A.M. with more barbed wire, ammunition, and two light machine guns, which proved that Gerber had been at least partially successful in getting the additional supplies. Sully Smith was noticeably disappointed by the absence of soap flakes, but seemed consoled by the discovery of three cases of Bouncing Betty mines at the bottom of the stack of ammunition crates.

Around eleven, Lieutenant Minh led a fifteen-man daylight patrol out about five kilometers, advised by Sergeant Bocker. They made a broad semicircular sweep about the west half of the camp, more or less following the river and looking for signs of enemy activity, but found nothing except a large number of blood trails going off through the jungle toward the Cambodian border.

In the camp, the men continued to strengthen the bunkers and walls, to set out the new wire to form a third perimeter and patch up the holes in the original two, to set out more punji stakes along the earthen walls and in the moat in front of the walls, and to repair and refit such weapons as could be repaired. Everyone was bone-tired.

Around noon, the Army C-7 Caribou transport finally arrived. It brought in over two tons of ammunition, four more .30-caliber machine guns, six BARs, two 60mm mortars, two 81mm mortars, two .50-caliber machine guns, and a collection of spare parts, extra barrels, and six cases of claymore mines. It also brought Captain Gerber.

A tired-looking First Lieutenant Bromhead met him as the plane landed. As they talked, an RF work detail under the supervision of Sergeant Clarke and Sergeant Phuoc unloaded the aircraft and got the supplies safely stored in bunkers.

"Colonel Bates told me you guys took a pasting last night, and from the looks of it, he wasn't kidding," said Gerber. "I didn't find out until this morning. I was out getting drunk and enjoying the company of a young lady, Sorry I missed the party out here."

"Me too, sir."

"How bad was it? Really?"

"Bad sir."

"Okay. You better brief me right away. I've been ducking Crinshaw all morning. He's going to be calling pretty soon, and I'd better have some answers for him when he does."

"He already called. Twice."

"Oh, ▬▬. What'd you tell him."

"I didn't. Seems we're having trouble receiving Saigon this morning. I believe Sergeant Lim has been indisposed with Captain Trang all morning. Sergeant Bocker is conveniently out on patrol, and the rest of us dumb peons just don't understand the intricacies of ionospheric telecommunications."

"▬▬▬▬."

"Yes sir. Exactly sir."

"What about Luong?"

"We lost Luong last night."

"Too bad about that. He was a good man."

"Yes sir. A few of them are damned good, sir. Washington's minding the radio."

"How about Cavanaugh?" asked Gerber, suddenly realizing the lieutenant had avoided mentioning the junior commo specialist.

"He was out in LP-1 with Luong and some RFs. Up near the bridge." Bromhead sighed. "They had a pretty tough time of it sir."

"How tough?"

"All dead except Cavanaugh."

"Is he hurt?" Gerber couldn't hide the concern in his voice. He'd already lost Schattschneider and Kepler was wounded.

"Not physically, sir. At least not bad. He's got some nasty cuts and a bullet crease or two, and Doc McMillan pulled a couple of pieces of shrapnel out of him, but nothing major got hit. Doc says if it were only for the wounds we might not even have to evac him, but, well . . ."

"Come on, Johnny. What is it you're not telling me?"

"Well, sir, the doc gave him a heavy sedative. He'll probably sleep till supper. When he didn't come in this morning, Sergeant Tyme and Sergeant Fetterman took a patrol out to find him. And they found him all right. Just sitting there staring off into never-never land, with Luong and all the RFs dead. Jesus, sir, there were sixty-nine dead VC lying all around the LP. Sixty-nine of them. That's seven more than we picked up this morning around the camp itself. I figure Charlie dragged away two or three times that many."

"Cavanaugh killed sixty-nine Cong?" Gerber asked slowly, unbelieving.

"Yes sir. Him and Luong and the RFs killed at least that many. Maybe more. Charlie hit their LP just after he attacked the camp. Fetterman said when he found him this morning, Cavanaugh had a bloody, broken carbine in one hand and a bloody E-tool in the other. They never did find that big Randall knife he always carried. And there wasn't a single round of ammunition left on any of them. Doc says Cavanaugh told him the last three times the VC attacked them, they didn't have any ammo. They were using what they got off the Charlies the time before. Other than that, it was all hand to hand.''

Gerber whistled. ''You reckon we can get him a Distinguished Service Cross out of this?''

''I reckon we ought to try and get him the ~~goddamned~~ Medal of Honor, sir. But I suppose with Crinshaw sitting back there in Saigon we'll be lucky to get him a ~~goddamned~~ Good Conduct Medal. Uh, meaning no disrespect to the general, of course, sir.''

''I understand how you feel, Johnny. Well, we can try anyway.''

They were interrupted by the approach of Sergeant Washington. ''Captain,'' said the twenty-one-year-old staff sergeant. ''Glad to have you back, sir, but I don't think you're going to be glad to be back. Big Green is on the line again. General Crinshaw says if I don't find you and put you on the horn right now, he's going to personally fly out here and bust all of us incompetent upstarts all the way to civilian. Those were his exact words, sir.''

''Maybe we should take him up on it,'' offered Bromhead.

''Okay, Jeff. You go tell the general I just got in, and I'm on my way over. I'll be there in about five minutes.''

''General Crinshaw did say 'now,' sir.''

''I understand, Sergeant. Just tell His Highness I'm on my way.''

''Yes sir.'' Washington grinned.

As the medical specialist trotted back off toward the commo bunker, Gerber turned to Bromhead again. ''Any word on Sergeant Kepler? I tried to hunt him up in Saigon this morning, but nobody at the hospital seemed to know where he was.''

Bromhead burst out laughing. Gerber wondered for a moment if the strain of last night had been too much for the young lieutenant. Bromhead was laughing so hard he was holding his ribs.

''He came in on a chopper about half an hour ago. Not scheduled. He traded a CH-47 crew four bottles of Beam's to fly him down here from Nha Trang," Bromhead finally got out. "I think they were going to Saigon."

"What the hell was he doing in Nha Trang?"

"Nobody knows yet, although we can surmise. He had a 90mm recoilless and one hundred and fifty rounds of HE with him. At first I thought you'd sent it."

Gerber shook his head. "I couldn't get a ninety. I tried. But what's so funny about that?"

Bromhead broke into another fit of uncontrollable laughter. "Oh nothing sir," he wheezed. "But after we unloaded the ninety and the ammo, the pilot says to me, 'What about that?' And I look in the cargo bay, and there's Derek, asleep on the deck, with his head propped up against a case of Beam's, an empty bottle in one hand and his M-14 in the other, drunk as a skunk and out like a light."

"Yeah, but I still don't see what's so damned funny."

Bromhead doubled up in another spasm and pounded on his own knee. Finally, he got out the rest of the story. "It was the clothes, sir. He was wearing a dress. A white nurse's dress, with his web gear on over the top of it, and his booney hat. And nylons, Captain. I swear to God. White nylons with his jungle boots on over them, and a bra."

"No shit?"

"I shit you not, sir. Nylons, a bra, and the nurse's uniform with his web gear on top, and his OD skivvies underneath."

"Does anyone know about this?"

"I imagine everyone does by now, sir."

"Well, let's hope Crinshaw doesn't. I wonder where he got the ninety?"

"Guys in the chopper said he told them he stole it."

"Oh, God. Did they say from whom?"

"Sorry." Bromhead shook his head. "All they said was he said he liberated it from some candy-asses who didn't need it."

"I don't believe it," said Gerber. "I go to Saigon for one day, and while I'm gone, my camp gets hit by a reinforced VC battalion, Crinshaw chews my ass, and my Intell sergeant, who's supposed to be in Saigon healing his wounds, is up in Nha Trang stealing a recoilless rifle and trying on nurse's clothes. Johnny, is this what happens when I leave you minding the store?"

"Sorry, sir." Bromhead smiled. "I just thought we were doing pretty good, considering. After all, I am just a lowly first lieutenant."

"Can't expect a boy to do a man's job, I suppose," teased Gerber. "Was he really wearing nylons?"

"And a bra, sir."

"And a bra. Oh well." Gerber sighed. "At least we'll have some bodies to show His Imperial Highness Crinshaw, for the royal body count."

Bromhead's grin vanished. "Uh, well, sir, there might be a little bit of difficulty about that."

He stuck a thumb over his shoulder and pointed across the camp to where a cloud of thick, black, oily smoke was beginning to roil up near the new outer wire.

"Oh, no, Johnny. Tell me you didn't," said Gerber as the stench hit him.

"Not me, sir. At least not entirely. Actually, it was Sergeant McMillan's idea. He pointed out that they were already beginning to create a health hazard, and there were just too many of them to bury while we were trying to get the camp fixed back up. Sergeant Fetterman agreed, and well, sir, I didn't want to do it, but I had to, given the situation."

"I hope you at least took pictures."

"Sir!" Bromhead sounded genuinely shocked. "What kind of ghoul do you take me for?"

"Christ. There goes Cavanaugh's DSC."

"Up in smoke, sir?"

"Metaphorically speaking. Come on, Johnny. We're

going over to the commo bunker. You've got till we get there to figure out what I'm going to tell Crinshaw.''

"I don't suppose we could credit them KIA to the air force and claim the napalm burned 'em all up?"

"Even Crinshaw isn't stupid enough to believe that.''

"No." Bromhead sighed. "I suppose not."

CHAPTER 10 _____

"Before we get under way with the briefing," said Gerber, "I thought you'd like to know that Sergeant Cavanaugh is doing okay. Sergeant McMillan informs me that he's been in contact with the doctors back in Saigon, and they report that Sean has come completely out of his catatonic state and, although still suffering from acute fatigue, is talking and responding well to treatment. They're optimistic that he may eventually be able to return to full duty, although they aren't saying just when."

There was a general murmur of relief from the assembled men.

"Because there were no surviving witnesses to the action at LP-1," Gerber continued, "the Congressional Medal of Honor is out of the question, which is too damned bad, but that's the way it is. You've got to have witnesses for the CMH."

"But sir, there were no witnesses because everybody else was killed," interrupted Bromhead. "It just isn't fair."

"I know it isn't fair, but that's the way it is. I've spoken with Colonel Bates, however, and he's assured me that he will forward my recommendation for a DSC for Sean to MAAG with all possible dispatch, and with his personal endorsement. Colonel Bates himself would have preferred recommending the higher award, but pointed out that with-

out eyewitness testimony, the recommendation likely would
never get higher than MAAG.''

"You mean it wouldn't get past Crinshaw,'' said
Bromhead disgustedly. "That lousy candy-~~assed~~ chairborne
ranger.''

Gerber gave his executive officer a sharp look, but let it
pass. He could understand the young lieutenant's frustration.
Still, he would have to have a private word with Bromhead
later. It wouldn't do, either for discipline or for Johnny's
career, to let him go around making unflattering comments
about generals in front of the men. Not even if the comments were true.

"Okay, let's get on with it. It's no secret to anyone here
that Charlie wants us out of his backyard. The heavy
losses he took when he hit the camp three days ago only
made him that much more ~~pissed~~ off at us. Even Saigon
figures that old Charlie is going to give it another try soon.
While he's been licking his wounds and burying his dead,
he's also been building up his forces to hit us again. He
knows he's got to do it soon, because while he builds, we
build, and if he waits too long, he won't be able to take
this place no matter what he throws at it. Intell indicates
we can expect Charlie to have another go at us before the
week is out.''

An uneasy muttering spread slowly around the room.

Gerber continued. "In the interest of postponing Charlie's
visit a little longer, Sergeants Kepler, Tyme, and Fetterman
have come up with an idea that I've had to reluctantly
agree makes a certain amount of sense. It involves creating
a ruction in Charlie's front yard. I'll let them tell you
about it.

"Derek, it's your show.''

"Thank you, sir.''

Kepler crossed the floor of the briefing room and flipped
the canvas cover back over the easel, revealing a large-
scale map of the area on both sides of the border near the
camp. The map was an old one, made by the French, and

somewhat less than totally accurate. Kepler had improved it by carefully sketching in landmarks, villages, and other corrections, based on patrols conducted on the Vietnam side of the border and aerial reconnaissance photographs.

"By now, most of you will be familiar with the village of Moc Phoc, about six klicks north of here, and almost on the border."

He touched the map briefly with a wooden pointer.

"The village is headquarters for the local VC cadre, and was used as a staging area against this camp prior to the raid three days ago. Sergeant Fetterman and myself have run patrols into the village with Lieutenant Minh on two separate occasions and have taken fire from the village each time, but have not been able to kill or capture any VC or weapons. The Cong simply take a few shots at us, then scoot across the border into Cambodia, where they know we won't be able to follow them because of political repercussions. That leaves only old women, children, and old men in the village, who, of course, don't know anything about the VC. When we question them, they always say all the young men and women are working in the fields or have gone to other villages to look for work. The villagers never quite seem to be able to explain to us where these other villages are. Naturally, everybody is very loyal to the Saigon government, although most of them don't seem to have any idea who the Saigon government is these days. One old man did tell us he was glad that the Americans had come to help drive out the French."

That brought a chuckle from several in the room.

"Anyway," Kepler continued, "we've been keeping the village under observation, and our scouts report a buildup is underway. Right now, there are about thirty-five or forty local guerrillas in the village, and about a company of main-force VC. This is not good.

"Across the border, about two klicks to the southwest, is a major VC encampment near what used to be the village of Bang Me. When the village was abandoned about ten years ago, the 123rd Independent Viet Cong Battalion moved in and established a permanent camp there. Intell figures it was the 123rd that hit us three days ago. According to photo intell, there's been a flurry of activity in there since the attack on this camp. Estimates are that the 123rd is at or near full strength. Impressive, considering the damage we inflicted on them and how quickly they've bounced back. Also not good.''

Kepler had everyone's full attention now. The men sensed that the worst news was yet to come. They were right.

''Now this,'' Kepler continued, circling an area on the map southwest of Bang Me and almost directly west of the Special Forces camp itself, ''is the hamlet of Lop Nhut. It's about ten klicks inside Cambodia. It's also been identified by photo intell as a forward staging area for the VC main-force AWF regiment. Obviously the 123rd is drawing replacements from the camp, and is preparing to hit us in conjunction with part or all of the AWF.''

The silence that followed in the briefing room as Kepler handed the pointer to Sergeant Fetterman and returned to his own chair, was absolute.

''Now what most of us would do in such a situation is request immediate reinforcements, which is exactly what Captain Gerber has been doing for the past two days. Captain Gerber requested a battalion of South Vietnamese Rangers be sent to reinforce us. The request was denied. Then he requested a battalion of South Vietnamese Marines. The request was denied. Same for ARVN infantry. Same-same for an ARVN 105mm battery, or a tank platoon. MAAG seems to feel that we're lucky to be receiving the additional machine guns and mines we've requested. Apparently they remain unconvinced that the level of hostile activity in the area is sufficient to merit the commitment of additional manpower, the fact that we probably would have lost the camp three days ago without TAC Air not withstanding.

"Subsequently, Sergeant Tyme and myself formulated a plan that hopefully, will tend to slow the VC down a bit. The plan was at first rejected because of its unorthodox nature, but in light of the problem with obtaining additional troops, Captain Gerber has reconsidered. What we plan to do is, ah, get the VC to give us a hand killing them.

"Tomorrow evening, Sergeant Tyme and myself are going to take half our Tai strikers and go for a little walk. We figure about 0200 hours, we ought to be in position to disturb the sleep of our friends over Bang Me way."

"You gotta be joking," said Bromhead.

"Lieutenant, when it comes to killing communists, I never joke."

"What can you seriously hope to accomplish against a main-force battalion with two platoons of light infantry? All you're going to do is piss them off."

"That's all we want to do. It would be nice to kill fifty or a hundred of them in the process, but if we only make them mad enough to chase us, that'll be sufficient."

A strange expression crossed Bromhead's face, a mixture of disbelief and understanding. "Why would you want them to do that?" he asked.

"Lieutenant, I thought you would never ask.

"While we're waking up the 123rd, Lieutenant Minh is going to be throwing up a partial perimeter around three sides of Moc Phoc. When he moves into the village with his company of RF strikers, the VC there will, we hope, run true to form and hotfoot it back across the border into Cambodia, after taking a few shots at Minh's people. The plan won't work if they stay and fight, but given their previous performances, we don't think they will. They wouldn't want to jeopardize their careful buildup of manpower and tip their hand about the upcoming assault on our camp.

"When the VC go skipping merrily across the border into their presumed safe haven, they're going to run smack into an ambush, carefully orchestrated by Captain Gerber and Sergeant Kepler and the remainder of the Tai strike company. This is going to make them mad as hell, and hopefully, they will also be mad enough to chase Captain Gerber and his Tais, particularly since they'll be chasing him away from the border, and deeper into Cambodia, which as the captain has already said, they regard as their front yard.''

He indicated an area of dense brush, but few trees on the map. "At this point, Captain Gerber's team will break contact and slip away to the south. The VC will be encouraged to keep moving forward by the presence of several firefight simulators that Sergeant Smith and myself have been improvising out of some demolition blocks, a few grenades, and a couple of thousand firecrackers. We will have emplaced the simulators on our way to visit the 123rd. The simulators can be triggered over a short distance by a radio signal broadcast on a certain frequency. Captain Gerber will have one transmitter, set to trigger half of the simulators, and Sergeant Smith, who will be with Sergeant Tyme and myself, will have a second transmitter, set on a different frequency to trigger the other half of the simulators. If all goes according to plan, we will reach the AO at approximately the same time as Captain Gerber's team, trigger our simulators, and also evade to the south. With a bit of luck, the VC company from Moc Phoc and the 123rd, both of them following the sounds of the simulators, ought to come together just about here, at around 0300 hours, and annihilate each other.''

"What if they don't," Bromhead objected. "What if they're smarter than you think, and they just drop back to the river and wait for you to try to come on across the border?''

"Then they'll have a long, lonely wait," said Gerber, "because we won't be coming back across the border. Instead, we'll be swinging southwest toward Lop Nhut.''

"Have you gone out of your mind?" asked Bromhead.

"Possibly."

"Sir," said the lieutenant seriously, "you can't be planning to hit the AWF. Trying to fight a regiment with a company makes about as much sense as going tiger hunting with a jackknife."

"I don't intend to fight them, Johnny, but I do intend to hit them. Just hear out the rest of the plan, will you?"

"With all respect, sir, this isn't a plan, it's suicide."

"Lieutenant," said Fetterman slowly, "I'm going to take good care of the captain here. Besides, you don't think I'd be a party to anything that'd keep me from going home to Mrs. Fetterman and the kids, now, do you?"

Bromhead glared at him, but said nothing.

Gerber gestured for the master sergeant to continue with the briefing.

"Once the two strike forces have linked up, we'll swing southwest to Lop Nhut as Captain Gerber indicated. We will attack the camp from the east and north, at 0430 hours, using automatic weapons, mortars, and bazookas. The attack will last for precisely four and one half minutes. Any longer than that might give them time to put together a reaction force and come looking for us. After the attack, we will head straight east toward the border for a couple of klicks, then swing well to the south, and cross back into Vietnam here, below the camp.

"The overall program should, at the very least, shake the Cong up pretty good. With a bit of luck, any reaction force from the regiment might keep heading straight for the border, figuring that's what we'd do, and run into what's left of the 123rd just about dawn, inflicting a few more casualties among themselves before they sort out what's what.

"In the meantime, Lieutenant Minh will have moved his company out of Moc Phoc, after a cursory search of the village, back to the camp to pick up additional equipment, and then down here to this point below the camp. He'll have Doc McMillan and a couple of Vietnamese medics with him, as well as Sergeant Tam, the LLDB assistant medical specialist. Lieutenant Minh will be deployed in such a fashion as to be able to assist us if we have any difficulties recrossing the border, and will have one of the 81mm mortars and the 90mm recoilless with him, along with one of the new .50-calibers, to provide such supporting fire as may be necessary.

"Mission sterility will be partially affected by using some of the weapons we've captured from the VC so far. We've picked up one RPD, about a dozen AK-47s, some Chicom Type 43s and 50s, and several Thompsons and Stens that the Cong apparently got from the French, who got them from us and the Brits. There's also a couple of MAT-49s, two BARs, and a bunch of SKS and MAS carbines. The real problem isn't a shortage of sterile weapons, but of sufficient magazines and ammunition for them. The captured stuff will be augmented by M-2 carbs and Thompsons from our own supplies, since they've been spread around the world so much we can consider them sterile for this mission. The VC use them all the time.

"The two strike forces crossing the borders will be totally equipped with automatic weapons due to the nature of the mission. We'll also be taking a disproportionately high number of BARs and four .30-cal. Brownings, four 3.5-inch rocket launchers, and two of the 60mm mortars. We'll just have to be careful not to leave anything too obviously American behind in the field," Fetterman finished.

"You don't seriously think we're going to fool anybody, do you?"

"Johnny," said Gerber, "Of course they're going to know who did it, and they'll scream bloody murder. We've just got to make sure they can't prove who did it. And then deny it anyway."

"What are you going to tell Saigon?"

"I don't know. Bates will understand, I'm sure of that."

"And Crinshaw?"

"American forces are prohibited from entering Cambodia.

Therefore, I won't be able to tell him anything about some rumors of fighting in Cambodia. Can't know anything about that if I wasn't there."

Bromhead snorted.

"That'll go over like a lead zeppelin. How're you going to explain friendly casualties?"

"We encountered a large VC force south of the camp, on this side of the border."

"What are you going to show the general for bodies?"

"Maybe we'll bring back a few. In any case, we'll have lots of captured weapons to show him. The ones we've got now. Look, Johnny, I don't say the plan is perfect, or without risk, but you know as well as I do that we can't repel another major attack yet. Not until we get our defenses really beefed up. This operation could buy us the time we need."

"It could also get you and about half the team killed."

Gerber rubbed his eyes. He'd expected some resistance to the plan, but not this much, and certainly not from Bromhead.

"In which case, Lieutenant, you will be faced with the very unpleasant prospect of explaining just what in the hell went wrong to the general. Come on, Johnny, we have to try something. Besides, we're supposed to be unconventional, remember?"

"Yes sir. I suppose we do have to try something." Bromhead sighed. Then he grinned and shook his head. "Boy. Crinshaw sure isn't going to like this."

"He ain't going to like it," grunted Fetterman. "What about the Cong?"

CHAPTER 11 _____

The immediate problem of what to do about Captain Trang had turned out not to be a problem at all. Gerber had merely pointed out that it was necessary to go into Saigon to requisition some additional supplies for the camp and that he really didn't have the time to do it himself. Trang, always eager for any excuse to go into Saigon, had immediately volunteered to help the poor, overworked American captain. Gerber had graciously accepted the offer, and Trang had left right after breakfast, taking Sergeants Lim and Hinh with him. Before departing, he had informed Gerber in an embarrassed tone that it was just possible that what with obtaining the supplies in addition to a number of official errands Trang would have to take care of in Saigon, it was just possible that well, they might have to spend the night in Saigon and come back the following day. Gerber said he understood, thanked Trang for his help and for the sacrifice of his valuable time, and saw him off on the morning helicopter, glad to be rid of the man.

The rest of the day was spent in familiarizing the Tai strikers with the captured VC weapons and in conducting live firing exercises of twenty or so men at a time. Lieutenant Minh, who had been told only part of the plan, more to protect him from having to answer awkward questions later than out of any real worry about a security leak, said nothing to Gerber about all the unusual activity, but watched everything with amused interest. At lunch, he wished Gerber, "Good luck, and good hunting." And then said no more, except to assure him that he'd be waiting at the designated RP south of the camp to assist them when they came back across the river. Minh carefully avoided using the word "border." At that point, he knew, the border was less than a hundred meters from the west bank of the river.

Bromhead had been both relieved and angered when Gerber had told him the part he was to play in the adventure. He still thought the plan very risky, both politically and militarily, and was glad that he wouldn't be going into Cambodia himself. He was also angry about being left out of the action, and a little concerned that Gerber's decision to leave him in charge of the camp was a reflection upon his combat prowess, really his courage, that had been brought about by his objections to the plan. Or worse, that the men might interpret it as such.

The reasons for leaving him behind, were, however, carefully thought out and sound in terms of both the military and the political situation.

"First, I don't want any more Americans crossing the border than absolutely necessary, in case we do run into trouble," Gerber assured him. "Second, we've got to get the Vietnamese in on the act, so that Saigon can't accuse me of running my own little war out here like some damned cowboy, and that means Lieutenant Minh has got to go to Moc Phoc and then down to the RP. Third, with two companies out, and a lot of the automatic weapons, part of the mortars, and all the rocket launchers missing, the camp is going to be pretty thinly defended. I need a good man in charge, and you've already proven that you're a good man to leave in charge. If you have the slightest inkling that the camp is going to be hit while we're out, call TAC Air first. They'll be able to do a lot more for you than we will, and a hell of a lot faster too."

Bromhead nodded his agreement as Sergeant Tyme came up.

"Got your weapon right here, sir," said Tyme, handing Gerber a submachine gun and a set of black VC web gear hung with fifteen magazines.

"Swedish K?"

"Yes sir. Karl Gustav M-45B 9mm. We had three of them in our own sterile stock. I gave Sergeant Fetterman the suppressed one. He wasn't happy about leaving behind that M-3 of his, but he didn't seem to mind too much."

"What about grenades?" Gerber asked.

"Put half a dozen in an empty canteen cover for you, sir. Right there on the belt. I'm afraid we had to make some concessions of sterility to common sense, there. We didn't recover too many unexploded grenades. Most of those we did were Chicom stick grenades that were duds. There were a couple of Soviet-made F-1s, but when Sergeant Smith and I got to checking them over, we found the time delay on the fuses varied all the way from thirteen seconds clear on down to zero seconds."

"Zero delay?" Gerber asked amazed.

"Yes sir. No delay. I suppose they're designed for boobytrapping, but evidently, the Charlie carrying them didn't know that. He blew himself up with one. It's something to think about, if you pick one up in the field, before using it. Also the damned things make a noise when the fuse arms that'll scare the crap right out of you. We fixed that by replacing the fuses with U.S.-made ones. They seem to be fully interchangeable with either the Mk II or the M-26. Kind of makes you wonder what else is. Anyway, we decided on using Mk IIs for the most part—the whole grenade I mean. They're not as efficient as the M-26, but they've been around so long and so many countries have used them that they're practically sterile.

"Sergeant Smith has improvised a number of claymores out of TNT blocks and those spike nails you got him. Not as effective or convenient as the issue model, but still very nasty. He's improvised both electrical and mechanical firing mechanisms for them. They ought to be fairly good for discouraging pursuit if Charlie gets too close on our tail."

"Let's hope so. Most of the other preparations coming along okay?"

"Yes sir. Everything's shaping up nicely."

"Okay. Once things are in order, I want everybody going out tonight to get some sleep, especially the team members and the Tais. Make sure Lieutenant Bao gets the message."

"Right sir."

"And, oh, Sergeant, I hate to tell you this, but you'll have to leave your shotgun behind. It's about as identifiable as you can get."

Tyme looked hurt. "I realize that sir."

"So? Are you taking the other K?"

"No sir. I gave that to Sergeant Kepler. I've been itching to try one of the Soviet AKs. They have more range and shock power than an SMG, and a couple of those we recovered have a flip-up luminous post for night firing. The workmanship is kind of crude, and of course they haven't been too well maintained, Charlie just doesn't seem to understand the importance of a clean weapon, but Sergeant Smith and I found a couple of good ones. They're reasonably accurate and seemed to function reliably after we gave them a thorough cleaning."

"Okay," said Gerber. "I'll see you later."

"With respect, sir, your orders were for everyone to zero in the weapon he'd be using before we went out, and you haven't fired yet."

"You win," said Gerber. "How soon will you be ready for me?"

"Sergeant Fetterman is holding a spot open for you now, sir."

"Okay, then, let's go down to the range."

He left Bromhead to see after the details of the camp.

*   *   *

They moved out after dark, in three separate groups, the Americans and Tais wearing a motley collection of tiger-striped fatigues, black pajamas, and dark blue civilian shirts and slacks, the Vietnamese strikers under Lieutenant Minh garbed in issue tiger-striped jungle suits.

In addition to his individual weapons and equipment, each man going into Cambodia carried either three rounds for the 60mm mortars or three rockets for the bazookas in his pack, and an extra belt of ammunition for the .30-caliber machine guns. Each team took two PRC-10s to assure reliable communications, although the radios were to be used as little as possible. This, added to the firefight simulators and their radio triggering devices, improvised claymores, flares, grenades, and other necessary items, made each man's load in excess of fifty pounds. Some men carried much more than that. Most of it would be expended in Cambodia.

At precisely two A.M., a half-dozen rifle-grenade-launched parachute flares burst over the village of Moc Phoc, and Lieutenant Minh's troops moved into the village, shouting and firing their carbines and Garand rifles. Return fire from the village was a bit heavier than normal, but, as in the past, the VC in the village rapidly broke off the engagement, crossing the border into the imagined sanctuary of Cambodia.

As they attempted to cross the river at a wide, shallow point directly opposite Moc Phoc, Gerber gave the order to open fire. As he did so, Kepler, Lieutenant Bao, and three designated tribesmen fired parachute flares from hand-held projectors, illuminating the killing zone. With a large number of VC caught in midstream, in the shallow water, the effect of grenades and two platoons of automatic weapons was devastating. In fact, the ambush was almost too good, and Gerber had to order a cease-fire early, in order to prevent killing so many of the VC that they wouldn't be inclined to give chase. Predictably, the Tais were reluctant to quit firing, but as the flares sputtered out and targets became hard to see, Gerber was finally able to get the strikers moving away from the river. Gerber estimated the ambush had probably killed or wounded thirty or thirty-five VC, without any loss to the Americans or Tais. Kepler's estimate was somewhat higher.

As they drifted away from the river, Gerber hung back with the rear squad, making sure that they fired off a few rounds every couple of minutes, so that the VC would know where they were and be able to follow. After about twenty minutes, the two Tai scouts Gerber had left behind near the riverbank caught up with the rest of the unit, breathing heavily. They informed him that part of the VC had stayed behind to take care of the wounded, but that a force of about sixty or seventy men was following. The plan, at least so far, had worked.

In a long disused cemetery that had once lain at the edge of the village of Bang Me, the tiny settlement now only a dusty red memory, Master Sergeant Fetterman crouched behind a weathered, vine-smothered headstone and studied the Viet Cong camp two hundred yards away through a pair of night glasses.

The night was alive with the sound of crickets and night birds and the whine of the ever-present mosquitoes, and somewhere off to the left, something large and heavy sounding rustled through the brush.

Probably a deer or a tapir, thought Fetterman. I wonder where the dogs are. Every damned village in Southeast Asia has dogs, but I don't hear any. There ought to be dogs.

But there were no dogs. There was only the coughing, popping gasps of the asthmatic, ancient gasoline generator that powered the camps few dimly flickering lights.

There were a half-dozen small thatched bamboo huts, probably offices or officers' quarters, facing a dozen long-houses set a foot or two above the ground on stiltlike pilings: the barracks. Between them was a fairly large packed dirt parade ground, with a fairly low, bamboo watchtower in the center. There was a single, bored-looking guard in the tower, and beyond it, off to the side at the far end of the parade ground, was another long building that might have been a mess hall or another barracks. Next to it was an open-sided shed where the generator wheezed noisily, like an old man with emphysema. A fence of bamboo surrounded three sides of the camp and most of the fourth, obviously intended more to keep the men from wandering off than to keep out a large, well-armed attacking force.

I guess the Cong must figure they're pretty secure here, with their Cambodian friends ready to make a big fuss at the slightest hint of an American move toward their sanctuaries. It would be so easy to take these guys. Maybe we should have settled for wiping out the 123rd, Fetterman mused.

But while eliminating a VC battalion would have been easy enough from the look of the camp, it wouldn't, he knew, have done anything about shaking up the main-force AWF regiment, and if they were going to buy enough time to fortify the Special Forces camp sufficiently to repel the inevitable mass attack, they had to shake up the AWF.

A slight smile crossed Fetterman's lips, and he leaned to one side to whisper in Tyme's ear. "Find Krung and tell him to have two of the rocket launcher teams try for the generator shack with their last round."

Tyme's grin was briefly visible in the darkness. He understood. Here, in country that the Viet Cong had controlled for decades, Charlie would always be able to find replacements for the men he lost, and probably fairly quickly, for some time to come. But the generator, old and feeble as it was, was almost priceless. It could be years before the VC would be able to replace it, given that most of their supplies had to come down from North Vietnam by bicycle or foot porter. They might never be able to replace it.

Tyme slipped away into the night to find Sergeant Krung and the bazooka men.

There was no need for flares to illuminate the target. The four lights mounted on poles near the corners of the parade ground sufficiently lighted the area for the gunners, and a fifth light burned in one of the small hootches, probably the radio shack, if the VC had communications equipment. There were no obvious antennae, but an aerial could have been strung between the huts, or they might only have a small radio like the PRC-10s. After consideration, Fetterman instructed Smith to have one of the other two rocket launcher teams fire two extra rounds at the lighted window. If the first round was a hit, the team was to fire only one round, then fire the originally planned three rounds per launcher at the barracks, which were the prime targets.

Fetterman heard the faint crackle of distant firing, Minh hitting Moc Phoc, and then a few minutes later, more firing as Gerber sprang his part of the ambush. Almost instantly, he heard Gerber's voice, unnaturally loud in the quiet jungle, from the earpiece of the radio handset clipped to the lapel of the master sergeant's many-pocketed jungle jacket.

"Vladimir, Vladimir, this is Boris, Boris. We have contact. Proceed as planned. Repeat, proceed as planned."

"Roger Boris," Fetterman acknowledged. "Understand proceed as planned. Vladimir out."

Fetterman released the handset, letting it drop back against his shoulder, disengaged the safety on the Swedish K, and yelled, "Fire! Fire! Fire!"

His third shout was drowned out by the whoosh of the rocket launchers. As he took careful aim at the watchtower and emptied the magazine in six short bursts, the low smacking sound of the silenced submachine gun was lost in the roar as eighty light machine guns, BARs, AKs, and assorted carbines and submachine guns poured round after around into the enemy camp.

Two hundred meters is long range for a submachine gun, but Fetterman was delighted to see the flimsy bamboo tower shredded as rounds—either his or someone else's, it didn't matter—found the target. He was even more delighted to see the brilliant white flashes and thick smoke billow up from three of the barracks as the rocket launcher teams proved to be dead on target. The hootch with the light in the window vanished in a brilliant red and yellow-white ball as the fourth white phosphorus rocket sailed majestically through the open window and exploded with a shattering crash.

Definitely something hard in there, Fetterman judged by the sound of the detonation. Maybe they had a radio in there after all. Well, not anymore. Sorry, Charlie.

Although unable to hear his own weapon over the firing of the others, Fetterman knew it clicked empty by the feel. He quickly changed magazines and continued firing, emptying a total of three magazines and directing his fire at the burning barracks. There were fires all over the camp now, probably two-thirds of the barracks were ablaze from the white phosphorus rockets, and the light machine gun and BAR teams were having a field day, cutting down sleepy, confused, frightened men as they tumbled from the burning buildings.

Fetterman was appalled by the speed with which the VC organized a reaction force, despite the carnage in the camp. A single figure, undoubtedly an officer or high-ranking noncom, ran out of one of the smaller hootches and immediately began organizing the men around him. Fetterman fired a long burst at the man, but couldn't seem to get the range. He was sighting for a second try when the generator shack exploded and the camp lights went out. In the uneven light of the burning fires, targets suddenly became indistinct silhouettes that blended into shadow, leaped out stark against the background of flame, then were swallowed by the shadows once more. He switched his aim to the nearest of them, emptied the gun, and stuck in a fresh magazine, being careful to collect the ones he had emptied and stuff them back in oversized pockets of his jacket.

My God! he thought. How hellishly beautiful.

Then Tyme was at his elbow, giggling gleefully, like some silly junior high school girl, and Smith, a smile a klick wide on his face, was standing a few yards away yelling at them both to come on. It was time to go.

They had been loping through the dense brush for a good five minutes, moving quickly but not really running, and firing off a few occasional rounds, before Fetterman began to get that old prickly feeling along the back of his neck that told him they were being followed. Another five minutes and he was sure of it.

Well, that was what they wanted, so why wouldn't the prickly feeling stop? Fetterman knew the answer even before he'd finished framing the question. The people following weren't crashing wildly through the brush, firing blindly ahead of them at the fleeing Americans and Tais. They were moving quickly, but without uncautious haste, holding their fire so as not to telegraph their position and distance, content for the moment to play the game and follow the hunt.

Tyme fell in beside him.

"Think they're after us yet?" he asked.

"They're coming all right," Fetterman answered. "I can smell them. I'll bet I know who's leading them too. Just before we knocked out the generator, I saw this one guy trying to get a bunch of troops organized. I tried to kill the poor bastard, but missed. Wish I hadn't. This guy is good. He's got a tight rein on his men. They're being awfully quiet, back there, but they're there, all right. Better tell Sully to stretch it out a bit. These guys just might get a little closer than we want. I'm beginning to believe Intell was right about these guys being the ones who hit the camp, though I'm damned if I know how they bounced back so quickly after the pasting we gave them. But some of those dudes were good, and these guys on our tails are no slouches.''

Tyme nodded as he moved forward without a pause.

Gerber felt good. He was finally seeing some real action, finally doing his part for the camp. Of course, he gave it his best every day, but there was a difference between begging, borrowing, or stealing supplies, running smoke past Crinshaw and his little temper tantrums, and actually getting your ass out in the grass and twisting the curl in old Charlie's tail. The only thing bothering him now was how easy it had all been so far. The VC following them were a bunch of clods. That wasn't saying they were stupid, exactly. Just that they had been so secure in the area for so long that they'd grown complacent and careless. They were crashing through the jungle behind the strikers like a blind water buffalo, shooting at every shadow. The adrenaline was pumping through his body and he felt more alive than he had felt since Korea. Not even being with Karen had made him feel so good.

Karen.

He pushed her image quickly from his mind. Now was no time to be thinking about women, any woman. Especially her. Gerber didn't believe in love at first sight, but there was something about her. He didn't know what. He just knew that he liked her a lot, wanted to see her again. But not now. Now he must think about one thing only; the mission. The mission came first. The mission could buy the time to save the camp.

Fetterman's voice from the radio somehow managed to sound tinny and flat at the same time, informing him that the other team had reached the area of operations and would be initiating phase two of the plan. His usage of the term "condition yellow" was a warning that there was a potential problem, but that it had not developed into a serious one yet. Gerber wondered what the problem might be, and silently cursed himself for the limitations of the simple code they had agreed upon, but it could not be helped. They were inside Cambodia, and had no notion of the enemy's communications capability. To give specifics, in the clear, over the radio, without knowing who might be listening, was to invite disaster. Whatever the problem was, it would have to wait until the two raiding parties linked up.

When he was sure he was past the agreed-upon break-away point, he took the small, single-channel transmitter out of his pocket, extended the antenna, and flipped up the arming cover over the toggle switch. A small light above it glowed dully red, indicating the unit was ready to transmit.

Gerber flipped the switch and heard the first of the firefight simulators Sully Smith had sown through the area bang and pop and boom into short, noisy life. To Gerber it sounded exactly like what it was: a firefight simulator. He had a bad moment when firing burst out several hundred meters in front of him, then realized that it was Smith, triggering the second set of simulators. Evidently distance made a difference. It had fooled Gerber. He hoped it would fool the VC.

As the noise from both sham battles intensified, Gerber swung his two platoons southwest and moved three hundred meters as quietly as possible, then pushed hard for the rally point. Far behind them now, to the north, he could hear the sounds of more firing, the sporadic shooting of the VC who had been chasing them. They were still headed straight west and, if things went according to plan, should be encountering the troops chasing Fetterman's team at any moment.

Gerber found Fetterman and his men had already secured the rally point. The master sergeant was breathing heavily when he came up to him. They all were. Fetterman didn't waste words. "Some guys following us, seem to have their shit together. Good trackers. Quiet. I think we lost 'em, but I'm not sure. We'll know in a minute."

The men waited tensely, oblivious to the staggeringly humid heat of the night, the clouds of mosquitoes that descended upon them as soon as they stopped moving. For several minutes all was quiet, then there was renewed and prolonged firing from the north.

"That them?" Gerber asked.

Fetterman listened intently for thirty seconds, then shook his head. "Not enough firing. Also that bunch has lousy fire discipline. Must be a second bunch of them, or maybe they split up. Either way we got problems. Those clowns sure are shooting the hell out of each other, though."

"Think the firing will draw off the people following you?"

"I wouldn't bet a month's pay on it, sir. These guys are good. They do it by the numbers, just like they taught us at Benning and Bragg. If they're still following, and I'll bet they are, I'd say they're maybe twenty, not more than thirty minutes behind us. I got no proof, but they're there all the same."

Gerber had studied Fetterman's file, and in the process came to realize that he'd heard of him before. Following a narrow escape at the Bay of Pigs in Cuba in April 1961, Fetterman had spent a couple of years working with Montagnards in Laos. He was becoming something of a minor legend among Special Forces personnel. Gerber trusted his judgment, and his instinct. The man was a natural-born SCAF trooper.

"Recommendations?" Gerber asked.

"Hell, sir. The smart money says quit while we're ahead. We've already accounted for probably a hundred VC tonight. The way those jokers up north are going at it, the figures may well be closer to a hundred and fifty. Might be more than that. Plus whatever you guys knocked off."

"But you don't always play the smart money, do you, Sergeant?"

"No sir. And sometimes I lose my shirt too."

"But not when it counts. You're thinking we ought to go ahead and hit the AWF, aren't you?"

"Well, sir, that is what we came over here for, isn't it?"

"And what about those people you think are following us?"

"Hell, sir," said Fetterman. "If they're smart, they'll figure we're going to call it quits and run for the border. It'd take a crazy ~~sonofabitch~~ to believe we'd go on and hit the AWF that far inside Cambodia, with half the countryside up in arms against us. Besides, they already got some idea of how small we are. They must have. Otherwise we wouldn't have let any of them live, right? Of course, if the guy running that outfit is as crazy as we are, we could wind up getting our tail zapped just about the time we open up on the AWF, in which case we would be well and truly caught between a rock and a hard place." He shrugged. "You pay your piastre, and you take your chance."

"Meaning I'm the one getting paid to make the decisions?"

"More or less, sir."

"Okay, Master Sergeant," said Gerber. "Let's get the men moving. It's a long way yet to Lop Nhut, and our people didn't lug all that ammunition, mortar shells, and rockets this far just to carry them back across the border."

"Airborne, sir!" Fetterman said happily.

As the sergeant walked away, Gerber noticed something odd about the way the man moved. His step had a kind of bounce to it that hadn't been there before. He seemed almost jaunty. A middle-aged Peter Pan in combat gear.

I trust this man, thought Gerber. I like him. Even his brusque manner. Yet he's a walking contradiction. Everything about him is. A little guy who carries twice as much as anybody else without being noticeably strained or slowed down. Careful to a fault about wearing his flack jacket and helmet, yet this whole madcap scheme to take the pressure off the camp was his idea. He shares the credit with Justin Tyme, but I know it was largely Fetterman's plan. And when any sane man would be anxious as the devil to get back to the camp, he wants to go ahead and have a go at a main-force regiment, with a force of one hundred and sixty men, and no supporting fires. I hope I made the right choice. There's something definitely weird about this guy!

After the action earlier that night, the raid on the AWF regiment, when it finally came off, was almost a disappointment.

If Charlie had a communications system, it wasn't working this night. When they got there, the camp was as quiet as a church.

The camp was huge. It had a real barbed-wire fence surrounding it on ten-foot poles. It was shaped like a giant triangle, with a watchtower at each corner. There must have been forty barracks. There were pens holding chickens and pigs, electricity from a diesel generator, and what appeared to be a hospital, outdoor lecture areas, and an obstacle course and physical training area. Gerber found it hard to believe such a facility could exist so close to his own camp. He half expected a couple of lambrettas to pull up to the main gate and discharge a load of poontang.

But security around the place was almost nonexistent. There were a few sentries walking post, but they seemed to be doing it more to keep awake than to guard against intruders. There was no evidence of regular patrolling, and when Fetterman scouted out the camp's one listening post, the three VC soldiers in it were sound asleep. Three quick bursts from Fetterman's silenced submachine gun saw to it that they never got the opportunity to wake up. Gerber would have liked to have taken one of them back for interrogation, but a private probably wouldn't have been able to provide all that much useful information, and it would have been damned hard to explain where he came from.

Gerber assigned one of his sergeants to each of the four platoons, and he and Lieutenant Bao positioned themselves with the two mortar crews.

On signal, everyone began firing. In the space of exactly the four and one half minutes Fetterman and Tyme had calculated would be necessary for the attack, the Viet Cong camp was hit with forty 3.5-inch white phosphorus rockets, over a hundred high-explosive 60mm mortar shells, and nearly thirty thousand rounds of automatic rifle, machine gun, submachine gun, and carbine ammunition. Gerber couldn't begin to estimate the damage they had caused precisely, but he knew it was considerable. He figured they had inflicted a minimum of one hundred more casualties, perhaps as many as one hundred and fifty, perhaps more than that. When they pulled out, it looked like half of Cambodia was burning down.

And then they ran. First east, then south, and then back east toward Vietnam. They ran until their hearts pounded in their chests and each breath became an agonizing gasp, each step a Herculean effort, the movement of immovable feet by the irresistible force of will alone. They would run a hundred steps, then walk fifty, then run a hundred more. When the dawn came up, they were within sight of the border and still running.

They ran right into the ambush.

Fortunately, it was a fairly small one. There couldn't have been more than fifteen or twenty men in it, and they seemed to have only one heavy automatic weapon, but they had a lot of AKs and grenades. Afterward, Gerber found himself strangely thankful for the grenades. They were the Chinese Communist stick-type grenades, and about half of them failed to explode. Those that did go off produced less than spectacular damage.

If they'd forgot about the grenades and just keep shooting, they probably would have killed more of us, Gerber thought.

As it was, they killed six Tais and wounded thirteen more. None of the Americans were hurt, but Fetterman took an AK round in the middle of the back, smack between the shoulder blades. The radio he was carrying, and its heavy battery, slowed the round down, and his flak jacket stopped it, leaving him momentarily stunned, with a large purple-red bruise, but otherwise uninjured.

The VC had chosen their position carefully and had the Americans and Tais effectively pinned down in a crossfire from the AKs, while the machine gun kept raking back and forth over them, inflicting the real damage.

The ambush came to an abrupt end when Lieutenant Minh radioed that he had them under visual observation from across the river and asked if they needed assistance.

Gerber got on his radio and directed fire from the 81mm mortar and the 90mm recoilless rifle into the ambush positions.

Minutes later, Lieutenant Minh appeared at the head of a platoon of RF riflemen with fixed bayonets while Gerber and the others tried to sort out what had gone wrong.

The wounded were immediately taken across the river to where Doc McMillan had set up shop with Sergeant Tam and the RF medics.

Gerber gave Minh a look of mock severity and asked the lieutenant if he knew where he was.

"But of course, old boy," said Minh. "I was number one in my map-reading class at Sandhurst. I'm exactly eight klicks south of our camp, give or take a few hundred yards, and have just engaged and thoroughly trounced a force of *beaucoup* VC. They'll probably give me a bloody medal for it. But don't you think we should discuss it on the other side of the, ah, river? Some of my chaps can't read a map quite as well as I can. We wouldn't want any of them straying across the border accidently, in their zeal to pursue the fleeing, hated VC, now, would we?"

Gerber laughed. Minh's flippant attitude was just the trigger he had needed to break the strain of the long night, the exhausting run, and now the ambush.

Using map coordinates for the Vietnam side of the river, Gerber called for medivac for the wounded and then requested airlift back to camp for the rest of the men. They were all exhausted.

In due course, he was informed that a South Vietnamese Air Force medivac was on its way.

Lucky we're not still taking fire, he thought. Saigon wouldn't send U.S. Army Aviation for medivac unless an American had been hurt, and the Vietnamese wouldn't land if Charlie shot at them, which he always did, if he was around.

"What about the air transport?" Gerber asked.

"Negative," he was told. "Big Green has denied your request for airlift."

"I understand," said Gerber. "Airlift is not available."

"It's not that it's not available, Zulu Six," said Bocker, relaying the message he'd received from Saigon. "It's just that it's denied. Big Green says you can't need airlift because there's no way you can be chasing VC, since we got no VC out here."

"Christ!" said Gerber. "Zulu Six out."

Minh shrugged. "We both have trouble with difficult superiors, old boy. Don't take it personally."

"I'm getting mighty tired of Crinshaw and his silly-assed little games," Gerber blurted out. "Fetterman! We got any bodies to show the general? Looks like we're going to have to carry them back to camp, if we do."

"Just one," called Fetterman. "But I don't think I want to carry him back. Don't think you're going to want to either."

Gerber walked over to where Fetterman and Tyme were standing. Tyme was looking at the hole in the back of Fetterman's ripped-up flak jacket, and Fetterman was looking at the hole in the ground that had been the VC machine-gun position before the 90mm had scored a direct hit on it. There was a twisted piece of barrel with a broken bipod hanging precariously from the end, a splinter of wood stock, and some curiously bent cases in a broken ammunition belt. A slightly smoking body lay nearby.

"You know," said Fetterman, "this dude held tight and kept us pinned while his buddies slipped away after the shelling started. He deliberately sacrificed himself so they could get clear. That takes some real balls.''

"He's the only one we got?" asked Gerber, astonished.

"He's it," said Tyme. "There's a couple of blood trails, but no sign of the others. Just a lot of spent brass. You know, these guys knew where to hit us, and just how to do it. How do you suppose they knew? How do you suppose they figured out just where we'd come back across?"

"Christ!" said Fetterman. "Who are those guys?"

"Well," said Gerber, "let's see who this one was anyway."

He rolled the body over and was instantly sorry he'd done so.

The woman had no face.

CHAPTER 12 _____

For nearly thirty minutes, Gerber sat in his hootch, staring at the wall, and letting the sweat drip down his face. He was too tired to move, almost too tired to breathe. But he felt very good. The operation was a success. A great success. He had bought the time he needed. Finally he forced himself out of the chair and opened his wall locker so he could get out a bottle of Beam's. It was his last, and nearly empty, but he didn't care. A success of this magnitude deserved a drink, even if it was the last that he would get for a long time.

With the bottle, Gerber walked to the door of the hootch so that he could look at the camp. It was taking shape quickly now. Almost ready. The regular fire control tower was up. The permanent structures were nearly complete and fully sandbagged. It would take a whole regiment to push them off the hill. A crack regiment that knew fire and maneuver, and that was willing to take a lot of casualties to do it. With air support, there was a better than even chance that Gerber and his strikers could stop the assault. It depended on the breaks.

Gerber stuffed the cork back in his bottle and turned. He put the bottle on the table made from the remains of a wooden ammo box. He pulled off the jungle boots and unbuttoned his jungle jacket. Sitting there, facing the blank wall, he realized just how tired he was.

There was a tap at the door, and he turned to look over his shoulder. The communications sergeant was there. "What can I do for you?"

"Just got a message from Big Green, sir. They're sending a major out to talk to us."

"They give you any idea what it might be."

"No sir. Just said to have you standing by. Gave the ETA as four zero. Didn't say much else and wouldn't answer any questions."

"Okay. Thanks. Let me know when they're about ten out. I'll be in here."

Bocker took a step forward, studying the young captain. He didn't want to say anything, but he was worried about Gerber's attitude. It wasn't like him to take news of intervention from Saigon so calmly.

"Anything else?" Gerber asked without looking toward Bocker.

"No sir. I was just . . ." Bocker stopped. "No sir. That's it."

When Bocker left, Gerber sat down on the cot, leaned against the wall, and put his feet up. He looked at the bottle of Beam's but decided it was too far away to be worth getting. He was feeling very tired. He knew what the major from Saigon would want. After Crinshaw had denied them airlift, and since they had requested it within a klick of the border, it was obvious that the major was going to be a one-man fact-finding investigation. See how many rules Gerber had broken and how many pieces of paper he could fill up explaining it all for the brass hats in Saigon.

With both hands, Gerber scrubbed at his face, feeling the stubble. His eyes felt as if someone had thrown two handfuls of sand in his face. His muscles ached. It was fatigue, pure and simple. Gerber had hoped to get some sleep because he needed to stay awake all night. Full alert even though he didn't think Charlie would be in any shape to mount an assault that night. But you never could tell.

*   *   *

Thirty minutes later Bocker found Gerber asleep, sitting on his bed, his feet still propped up. He stepped into the tiny room and said, ''Captain. They're almost here.''

Gerber came wide-awake at once, knowing immediately where he was and what was happening. He said, ''Damn. Didn't mean to go to sleep. Wanted to get a shower and shave before that major got here.''

''If you hurry, you still might have time.''

Gerber stood up. ''No, I'd have to hurry too much. No time to enjoy it. Besides, I'll bet you guys used all the hot water.''

Bocker laughed. ''Wasn't all that much, and besides, it was just barely warm.''

''Tell you what. Have Fetterman meet the major at the pad and bring him up to the team house. I'll be there waiting with the coffee. That way he won't think we're too impressed with his coming all the way from Saigon.''

Bocker nodded and left.

Gerber stood up, walked to the footlocker that was pushed into the corner, and opened it. He pulled out a clean, OD T-shirt and looked for a clean jungle jacket. There was nothing he could do about his boots. All he could do was hope that the major wouldn't be too much of a garrison trooper.

Cleaned up as best he could, Gerber walked slowly to the team house. To the northeast he could see a speck that was the helicopter from Saigon. Idly he noticed that the pilot was staying well clear of the area where the helicopter had taken fire a couple of days earlier. He doubted that it made much difference because he doubted that the VC who had fired were still there. Anyway, it showed that the pilots were sharing information even if no one else in Saigon was.

In the team house, Gerber walked to the coffeepot, saw that one of the young Vietnamese women, married to someone in the LLDB, was doing her best to straighten up the area. She had put a clean cloth on the main table, put napkins and cups by the coffeepot, and set out the creamer and sugar. Gerber smiled a greeting at her and poured himself a cup of coffee. He sat at one of the small tables, facing the door, so that he would see the major when he arrived.

From the outside, he could hear the chopper touch down, and through the open door, he could see the cloud of red dust kicked up by the rotor wash of the helicopter. Three minutes later, the major, followed closely by Sergeant Fetterman, entered the team house.

"Nice to see you, Captain," said the major.

Fetterman stepped between them and said, "Sir, this is Major Dumont. General Crinshaw sent him out."

Dumont turned and glared at Fetterman. "That will be all. Captain Gerber and I have a number of things to talk about."

For a moment, Fetterman didn't move. Gerber nodded slightly and Fetterman left. Gerber stood up and gestured to the chair opposite him. "Care for some coffee, Major?"

"This isn't a social call."

"I know that. I thought we could be somewhat civilized about this."

Dumont sat down and waited. Gerber looked for the Vietnamese woman, but she had disappeared, so he got up. He filled a cup and asked, "Cream or sugar?"

"Black will be fine."

Gerber set the cup in front of Dumont and then sat down.

Dumont took a drink, made a face to indicate that he didn't like the coffee, and then said, "I suppose there is really no reason to beat around the bush." He looked around the room to make sure they were alone and then said, "We've gotten a report that you have been operating in Cambodia."

Gerber studied Dumont over the top of his cup as he

took a long, slow sip of coffee. "Just what was the nature of this operation?" he asked innocently.

"You have been reported to have attacked at least two enemy units in a country that is officially neutral."

"Who made the report?"

"That's not important. The question is, were you operating in Cambodia? Before you answer let me remind you that you requested airlift just on this side of the border, not far from where the engagement took place."

"Alleged engagement," said Gerber noncommittally.

Dumont took a small black notebook out of the left breast pocket of his jungle jacket. He flipped it open and said, "Let me also remind you of your rights under Article 31 of the Uniform Code of Military Justice."

Gerber slammed his cup down, slopping coffee all over the table. "Okay, Major. Enough already. You know as well as I do that operations inside Cambodia are illegal. We are not to cross that imaginary line on the ground called the border. Makes no difference that the North Vietnamese, and the VC, can cross it at will. Makes no difference that with some kinds of artillery, they can stay in Cambodia and lob shells at us all day, and we're not supposed to shoot back. Now you blow in here with some song and dance about illegal operations in Cambodia and won't even give me the courtesy of telling me where the complaint came from."

"And that hasn't answered my question."

"No sir, it hasn't. But I find the question offensive. And even if I had been operating in Cambodia, I wouldn't be inclined to tell you."

"I suppose it would do no good to ask the rest of your team?"

"Go ahead and ask."

Dumont flipped to a blank piece of paper and made a note. "I could interview the Vietnamese. I'm sure that some of them would be happy to talk to me."

"Major." Gerber sighed. "Ask anybody anything you

want. Ask the Vietnamese. But remember that not many of them can read a map, and most of them don't recognize the difference between Vietnam and Cambodia. Thirty miles to the west is just thirty miles to the west.

"And I'm getting a little sick of trying to justify everything I do to Saigon. My only concern is to protect my camp. Anything I do is to that end. If we let the VC push us out of here, it will be impossible to ever get another foothold here. The locals will see the VC as invincible. After all, they are basically the same bunch who threw the French out of here ten years ago."

Dumont held up a hand to interrupt. "I didn't come here for a history lesson."

"I know that. Let me say this. You will uncover no evidence that my team or I have been operating in Cambodia. If someone shot up a bunch of VC, then I think we should try to find out who it was and pin a medal on him."

"I take it then that I don't need to count on your cooperation."

Gerber laughed. "What do you want? A signed statement that says I violated international borders in an illegal pursuit of the war?"

"Okay, Captain," said Dumont, pushing back his chair so that he could stand up. "I'll want to interview your men and talk to the Vietnamese officers."

"You'll find them working. Talk to them all you want. I'll have Lieutenant Bromhead have the Vietnamese officers meet you in their team house. You can interview to your heart's content. I'll be here when you finish."

"You understand, Captain, that I'll make a full report about your attitude when I return to Saigon."

"And when might that be? Do we have to arrange for your transport?"

"When I'm ready, I'll radio Saigon." Without another word, Dumont spun on his heel and stomped out.

Gerber sat at the table, took a deep breath, and sighed.

At war with the VC and the brass hats in Saigon. No way to win. Just try to stay ahead of everyone.

For three hours, Gerber sat in the team house, drinking coffee and trying to catch up on his paperwork. Fetterman visited him once to tell him that Dumont had talked to all the members of the team but hadn't learned anything from them. Each said that they had been involved in an operation near the border designed to buy some time before the big push, but each denied that they had been in Cambodia.

Just after Fetterman left, Bromhead came in to report that Dumont was now talking to the Vietnamese. They were all saying that they had just completed a patrol to the west of the camp, but that it had been in Vietnam. With a smile, Bromhead said, "Our friend Lieutenant Minh asked why they would fight in Cambodia when there were so many communists in their own country. I think that made quite an impression on Dumont. I don't think he believes that the Vietnamese have brains. He's never met one who is as sharp as Minh."

At dusk, after the team had eaten and before the alert was lifted, Dumont walked into the team house, looking for Gerber. He had overseen the placement of the troops during the alert and had then cautiously moved back to the team house to wait. Dumont pulled out a chair and sat down opposite of him.

"It's too late to get a flight out tonight. I take it you have a place for me to stay."

"Of course. Did you bring a weapon, or would you like me to find you one."

Dumont looked mildly embarrassed. "I didn't plan to be here overnight. If you could find me something, I would appreciate it."

At midnight, Gerber slipped out of bed, trying not to wake Dumont, who was sleeping in a cot pushed against the far wall. He was still wearing his boots and pants. He pulled his jungle jacket off the back of the chair, picked up his M-14, and stepped out to finish dressing. Dumont didn't know he had left.

Instead of going straight to the fire control tower, Gerber went to the commo bunker. Fetterman was sitting in an old lawn chair, his feet propped up on a table, a can of Coke in his hand. He was staring at the radio, as if he was trying to will it to speak. Gerber said, "Anything happening?"

Fetterman let his feet drop to the floor with a thud. "No sir. Last reports from the LPs were right on time, and they hadn't heard anything."

Gerber reached out, took the can from Fetterman, and took a deep drink. When he handed it back, he said, "I'm going up to the fire control tower and take a look around. If you see Lieutenant Bromhead, tell him to check on the Vietnamese positions. I'm going to be in the forward command bunker on the west wall later on. Tell him to stop by."

"Sure. I was about to head over to number-three pit. Bocker said that they were having some kind of problem with the tube."

"Shouldn't Kittredge look at it?"

"Should. But he's out with the LPs again."

Outside again, Gerber stopped long enough to look at the sky. There was a full moon, and for some reason Gerber thought of the term "bomber's moon." It meant that the sky and light conditions were the best for bombing raids. Gerber didn't have to worry about that, but he did wonder if Charlie would make use of the conditions. He decided that he would be surprised if he didn't.

He was halfway to the fire control tower when he heard the first distant plop. He shouted "Incoming" at Fetterman, who was just coming out of the commo bunker, and sprinted across the compound. At the base of the tower, he dropped to the ground and waited for the explosion of the mortar round. It landed somewhere near the middle of the compound. A second later there was another, and then a third. When it hit, Gerber leaped to his feet, scrambled up the tower. He grabbed the night binoculars, scanned the trees far to the east of the camp, looking for a clue to the location of the enemy mortar tube.

After only a minute, he heard another round fired and picked up a flash of light. He grabbed the field phone and said, "Pit one. Pit two. Four rounds HE, one-twenty-five degrees, six hundred yards, charge four. Fire when ready."

He watched the rounds from his tubes fall close to where he had seen the flash. A second later, a couple more enemy rounds fell harmlessly in the camp. Gerber continued to scan but could see nothing. Each of the LPs reported, but they hadn't seen or heard anything. It meant that the VC had managed to set up their mortar tube far enough away to escape detection.

About an hour before dawn, Gerber climbed down, figuring that there would be no more harassing fire. The VC would want the time to get away. That didn't mean they wouldn't leave one or two men behind with rifles to snipe, only that they would try to get the tube out of the area.

In his room, he found Dumont sitting in the dark, smoking a cigarette. Dumont said, "This happen often?"

Gerber set his rifle down. "Once or twice a night. They aim at the center of the camp, figuring, I guess, that at the very least, the rounds will drop on us. So far they haven't managed to hit anything of importance. Wounded a couple of the strikers, but even that was minor."

"You don't seem too concerned about it."

"Mortars are nothing," said Gerber. "Charlie can't really aim them, and they don't do much damage. I've seen them hit in the mud and create a crater only a foot in diameter. They don't have much penetration power. The only real danger is the shrapnel, and if you stay down, you should be okay."

"I'll be going back this morning," said Dumont, changing the subject. Although there was no light on in the room, he could see Gerber staring at him. "You'll have to go with me."

"I can't leave the camp now. That attack was just harassment but a major assault is building up. Crinshaw was ~~pissed~~ that I missed the last assault because he wanted me in Saigon. There's no reason for me to go there now."

"No reason, other than that the general said that I should bring you back to explain what has been going on. I guess I'll be able to say that there are VC in the area, after last night. But you'll still have to come with me. I'm going to try to get the air asset here about ten. Be ready then. You'll probably have to spend a day or two in Saigon, so bring a change of clothes."

"Oh, come on, Major. You can't really expect me to leave now. How's that going to look? Every time something happens at the camp, I've found an excuse to go to Saigon." He still hadn't forgotten the feeling in the pit of his stomach when he learned how bad the assault on his camp had been. Although it wasn't true, he felt that he had betrayed his men by not being there. Not one of them had said a word to him to suggest they felt that way, but Gerber still wondered about it. Now, with an enemy build up around the camp, he was again being ordered to Saigon.

"You don't seem to understand, Captain. You are going to Saigon. There is no room for argument."

"Then you'll have to provide that order in writing."

"I'm not writing anything. I'll have General Crinshaw order you to Saigon."

"Fine. Let him provide the written order."

"He won't sit still for something like that. You can't go demanding everything in writing when it suits you."

"Check your regulations, Major," snapped Gerber. "I have every right to demand written orders. Especially after you've advised me of Article 31. Crinshaw might not like it, but he will do it."

Dumont stood up, shaking his head. "I'll have the order ready by the time we board. Good enough?"

"That will be fine."

Dumont started for the door, but Gerber stopped him, saying, "I'm sorry, but you'll have to stay inside for the next forty minutes or so. We try to keep everyone at battle stations just before dawn to just after, to reduce the possibility of sniper attack. Try not to provide Charlie with an opportunity to take out a couple of people easily."

"Don't be ridiculous. Nothing is going to happen."

"Let me remind you, Major, that you are on my base, and you'll comply with the standing orders. We are not going to expose anyone to enemy fire unnecessarily."

Dumont fell back into the chair. "Okay, Gerber. You win this one. Just be ready to leave when the chopper gets here."

CHAPTER 13 _____

The flight to Saigon was without incident. Gerber was bothered by the ease with which the helicopter got to his camp. He knew that Charlie was out there, but no one fired at the chopper. That seemed to indicate that Charlie didn't want to tip his hand early. So Gerber sat in the back of the helicopter, heading to Saigon, and worried. Worried about the defenses of the camp, the impending attack, and leaving Bromhead in charge.

Of course, on paper, Bromhead was just an adviser. Operational command really belonged to Trang, but the Vietnamese officer was happy to let the Americans give the orders. He might complain about it later, but during the actual operation, he would be hard to find. Lieutenant Minh would be more than happy to take command and, in fact, tried to follow the lead of the Americans. His training at Sandhurst, the British military academy, made him a real asset. It was too bad that Minh wasn't in command of the Vietnamese.

But there was nothing that Gerber could do about it. If he tried to get Trang replaced, the whole of the Saigon power structure, from the president on down, would fall on him. And when they got done, the American ambassador, the commander of MACV, and finally Crinshaw would want to take a shot. Gerber was sure that even Bates would have to speak to him. It would do no good to complain about Trang. Besides, the fact was that Crinshaw was already mad about something else. Gerber didn't need to add fuel to the fire.

They landed at Ton Son Nhut, in nearly the same place that they had the last time. Gerber hopped out after Major Dumont, and as they walked across the grass to the terminal, two sergeants came toward them. The older, higher-ranking sergeant saluted and said to Gerber, "I'll take your weapon, sir."

Gerber took a step back, to add a couple of feet of distance between them, and slipped off the safety. "I think not."

"It's just routine, Captain. Nothing personal."

"Sorry, Sergeant. I was taught, as I'm sure you were, that I never surrender my weapon."

"Yes sir. But we'll just lock it up for you so that you don't have to worry about it."

"No, Sergeant."

"Come on sir. No one minds. Saves them having to hassle with it."

"I said no."

The sergeant looked at Dumont, who shrugged. For nearly a full minute the sergeant, who was almost forty years old and not used to having anyone tell him no, stared at Gerber. Finally he stepped aside, and said, "All right, Captain."

As soon as they got away from the sergeants, Dumont said, "That wasn't necessary."

"Look, Dumont, I'm getting a little tired of everyone around here trying to dead-file regulations. I'm tired of people trying to take my weapon away from me, as if I didn't know how to handle it. I'm tired of trying to convince everyone that the enemy is out there, near my camp, waiting for an opportunity to take it back. I'm tired of fighting with the people in Saigon to get the supplies and support I need. I'm tired of being called away every time there is a buildup so that it looks as if I'm scared. Now, as the final insult, some fat old sergeant thinks I should hand my weapon over because he wants it. No way."

"You're not going to win any friends here with that attitude."

"Friends here, like those sergeants, I don't need."

Ignoring this, Dumont said, "Let's get over to General Crinshaw's office."

"No sir," said Gerber. "First, I want to check in with Colonel Bates. That's following the proper chain of command. Then I will be more than happy to meet with General Crinshaw."

"You realize that I'm going to report all this to the general."

"Of course. But it's all proper military procedure. The general might not like it, but it is correct."

"I wouldn't tell him that," said Dumont.

They found a sergeant with a jeep who had been sent to meet them. Dumont gave him orders to take him to Crinshaw's headquarters and then take Gerber to Bates's office. They were actually in buildings that were separated by no more than one hundred yards. Gerber realized that Dumont subscribed to the theory that you never walked anywhere when you could order a sergeant to drive you.

Inside Bates's office, actually the reception room, Gerber picked up the field phone, spun the crank so that he got the switchboard, and said, "Nha Trang."

"Sorry sir, circuits to Nha Trang are down."

"When do you expect them to be up again?"

"Can't say. The engineers are looking into it now."

"Thanks." Gerber hung up. To the sergeant, sitting behind the desk, watching him, he said, "Colonel Bates available?"

"Yes sir. Go on in."

As Gerber opened the door, Bates said, "Now what the shit have you done?"

For the next hour, Gerber explained, in great detail, exactly what he had done and why. He told Bates, mainly because Bates wasn't a leg and might even understand; although he hadn't been a Green Beret his whole career, he understood how things sometimes had to be. So Gerber told him about the raid into Cambodia in an attempt to buy another week. "We need that time, Colonel. We're just not strong enough yet."

Bates sat behind his desk, his head on his hands, almost as if pretending he hadn't heard a word. Finally he said, "How much of this are you going to tell Crinshaw?"

"Everything except that we went into Cambodia. I can't be held responsible for two communist units shooting each other up. They're just trying to create an international incident to embarrass us."

"I don't suppose there is any way that this could come back to haunt us?"

"No sir. We left nothing in the field. Even if we had, it was all sterile equipment. Items that could be found anywhere. M-2 carbines, AKs, captured weapons, that sort of thing."

"Anyone see you. Meaning you white guys?"

"Wouldn't matter. We had all darkened our skin so that we wouldn't stand out, except for our size. We tried to stay concealed."

"Okay. I suppose you had better get over and talk to Crinshaw. I might warn you that he called just before you came in. Was mildly upset that you declined Major Dumont's offer of an immediate audience. I did my best to pacify him, but he's still carrying a case of the ass. Keep that in mind."

Back in Bates's outer office, Gerber grabbed the field phone and tried again. This time the operator put the call through. Gerber told the operator in Nha Trang that he wanted to talk to the evac hospital, and when he got the switchboard there, he said, "I'd like to talk to Lieutenant Morrow."

He heard a ringing at the other end and then heard a voice say, "Captain Baker's office. Specialist Renwoole speaking."

"Lieutenant Morrow, please."

For a moment there was silence and then, "This is Lieutenant Morrow. Can I help you sir?"

"No. But I am in Saigon," said Gerber.

"Mack? Is that you Mack?"

"Yes. Can you get to Saigon?"

"No. I don't know. I can't just drop everything. I . . ."

Gerber laughed. "Whoa. Slow down. I'm in Saigon for the rest of the day, and won't leave until tomorrow. I know that there are regular flights from Nha Trang. I was hoping you could grab one of them."

She hesitated. "I want to. I really do. But it's such short notice."

"I know that. I would like to see you, but if you can't get here, I'll understand."

"Can I call you back? Where will you be?"

He gave her Bates's office as a reference, and said, "I'll check in here for messages. Hope to see you."

The meeting with Crinshaw was even worse than he expected. He knew, from both Bates and Dumont, that Crinshaw was mad, but he had no idea that he would be as mad as he was. The second that he closed the door, he knew things were going to be very shaky.

Crinshaw didn't play his waiting game. The instant he saw that it was Gerber, he threw his pencil down, let it bounce to the floor, and then shouted, "Close the damn door."

Gerber did as told and moved to the middle of the room so that he could stand in front of Crinshaw's desk.

"Gerber, I just can't believe you. I just can't believe

you. An operation in Cambodia. The government at Phnom Penh has complained to Saigon and is threatening to go to the United Nations. The ambassador has called three times today. This is . . . this is . . . the . . ." Crinshaw stopped shouting and sputtered, losing track of what he wanted to say. His face had gone from red, to deep red, to purple. He rocked back in his chair, breathing deeply.

"I didn't go into Cambodia and attack anyone," Gerber protested.

"You really expect me to believe that. There have been several protests already."

"What's the proof?" Gerber demanded. "There is no proof. The VC are trying to get everyone to overreact. They're trying to get us out of there without having to fire a shot."

"Captain, you're very close to a court-martial. I have a report here from Major Dumont about your attitude. There is so much. I just don't know where to begin."

Gerber didn't know what to say. He felt a knot build in his stomach, turning his whole body cold. He was shaking and felt sweat burst on his forehead. "You're going to take the word of a bunch of communists over a fellow officer?"

"Don't pull that shit on me. Don't even try."

"There is not one shred of evidence that we were there. If anyone could prove it, we would be looking at it."

"Are you telling me that you weren't operating in Cambodia? None of your people were there?"

For the first time, Gerber felt that things weren't as bleak as he had thought. There was enough doubt in Crinshaw's voice to make Gerber relax slightly. He said, "From what we can gather, two units of VC or North Vietnamese, operating independently, ran into each other and opened fire. They're blaming us so they won't look completely stupid, and by blaming us, they think that they can stampede the Saigon government and Washington into moving the base. Good strategy, if it works."

"That still doesn't excuse you. Your attitude toward Major Dumont has been thoroughly unprofessional, as was your response to the mortar attack. He has reported that you didn't increase your alert status, that you only responded with a few rounds of mortar fire from your own tubes, and that there was no camp-wide warning. And you didn't even call for air support."

Gerber looked longingly at the chair that Crinshaw had neglected to offer him. Still standing in front of the desk, he said, "We were already at full alert, as we are every night after midnight. We didn't have an exact plot on the enemy tubes and can't afford to indiscriminately fire into the surrounding countryside, and since everyone was supposed to be alert, there was no need to issue a camp-wide alert. Major Dumont should get into the field a little more often and he would realize that a total response, such as he suggests, is exactly what Charlie wants. He wants to dictate our policies. I'm not going to let him."

"I don't know," said Crinshaw. His anger had dissipated. "I can understand your policies, given the circumstances. I think you could have used a little more tact dealing with Major Dumont. An explanation would have stopped part of his negative report."

"I don't want to speak out of turn," said Gerber, "but Major Dumont came in with his mind made up. He told me up front what he expected. I gave him every courtesy possible, without endangering my camp."

"We'll not criticize other officers, Captain. You're still skating on mighty thin ice here. You're not out of the woods by any stretch of the imagination."

"Yes sir."

Crinshaw stood up, moved to the air conditioner to turn it up. He pulled the blinds on his window, blinked at the bright light from outside, and let them fall with a crash, shutting out the sun. He turned, stared into Gerber's eyes, and said, "I don't like the way you people operate."

From the way he said you people, Gerber knew that he meant the Green Berets.

"It's just not military. You violate the regulations you don't like. You ignore orders and standard operating procedures. You steal equipment, and side with the Vietnamese. None of you, not one, is regular army."

There was nothing for Gerber to say. He knew that since Crinshaw was now getting to the Green-Berets-don't-operate-the-army-way speech, he would be allowed to leave soon. He tuned Crinshaw out, preferring not to hear it again. There was nothing he could say to convince Crinshaw that this was a new war. That there were no forts to capture, no territory to invade, no teepees to burn, no war parties to be attacked. It was a war that demanded support of the Vietnamese people. Not the corrupt officials in Saigon who were lining their pockets with American money, but the farmer in the rice paddy who didn't care who was in power as long as he was left alone to raise his family and live his life. That was the real key to this, and old-time military officers like Crinshaw didn't seem to understand it. That explained the harping on body count. When you couldn't mark your progress on the ground, you needed a yardstick of some kind, and the body count was becoming it.

Crinshaw had stood up again and was pointing to his uncovered, secret map. "You can understand everyone's concern, can't you? Your base is less than twenty klicks from where the battle took place. It is only logical to assume that you had something to do with it." Crinshaw sat down again and said, "All right, Gerber, get out of here. But don't be surprised if you receive official notice that a fact-finding commission is on its way out to see you. I think the ambassador is going to demand, at the very least, something like that."

"Tell them not to hurry."

"Now what the hell does that mean?"

"It means that we're expecting to get hit, badly, in the next couple of days."

"Let's not get dramatic, Captain. You've made your point."

"Will that be all?"

"I want you to hang loose the rest of the day. The ambassador might want to talk to you personally about this Cambodian thing, boy. I hope you're prepared to tell him all that you've told me. And I mean all."

"We ignore proper clearances and military secrets?"

"You may assume, Captain, that the ambassador is cleared to hear anything and everything that you could possibly tell him. You answer all his questions. You understand?"

"Yes sir."

"And let's watch those smart-alecky tones, mister. You might have come out of this smelling like a rose, but I've got an eye on you. You screw up once, it even looks like you've screwed up, and your ▆▆▆ is mine. You got that, boy."

"Yes sir."

"Now get out of here."

Gerber got.

Back in Bates's office, he tried to call Karen but was told that she had left for the day, and the specialist there didn't know where she had gone. When he hung up, he turned to the sergeant in Bates's office and asked if there had been any messages for him.

"No sir. Not a thing."

An hour later, Karen walked in wearing dirty jungle fatigues, her lieutenant's bar pinned to the pocket, just above the Vietnamese rank equivalent. Gerber leaped up and was about to grab her when he remembered where he was. Instead, he stepped to her and took her hand. "Hi."

"Hi yourself," she said. "You have to stay here?"

"Nope." He turned to the desk and saw the sergeant

there smiling. To him, Gerber said, "We'll be at the club for the next hour or so. I should be in my quarters after that if anyone needs me."

Outside the door, in a corridor that was momentarily empty, Karen grabbed him and spun him so that he was facing her. Without waiting for him, she kissed him, hard. Then she stepped back and said, rather breathlessly, "Let me look at you."

A moment later, he said, "I could use a drink."

She studied him closely and then said. "Has it been rough?"

"You mean in the field or here?"

"Which is worse?"

"Here. Out there I know what to expect. I mean, there are rules, almost, and everyone plays by them. I know that if I do my job right, if I watch myself and don't make a mistake, I can survive. But here. Shit. I just don't know. Everything seems backward." He laughed. Snorted really. "No. It's worse here because you don't know who the enemy is. Except that it might be everyone."

At the club, Gerber ordered a Beam's Choice, downed it in one gulp. He slammed the glass on the bar, waited while the bartender poured another, and did the same thing. "Boy, that's smooth." Then he turned to Karen and said, "Sorry. But I needed that. Now I'll slow down. You want a screwdriver?"

At the table, they sat talking, laughing, trying to ignore the army/air force atmosphere. They ordered dinner, ate it slowly, and then danced for a while.

As they walked back to the table, Gerber said, "I never thought I would be dancing with someone in fatigues. But then, you do something for them."

Karen smiled and said, "What are we still doing here?"

"Dancing."

"Why?"

"Because I didn't want you to think that I was only interested in you for one thing. That I found you exciting

because you're intelligent, because you can think for
yourself. And it doesn't hurt that you're probably the most
beautiful woman I've ever seen.''

"Can we get out of here?''

"Thought you'd never ask.''

In less than ten minutes, they were in his room. Gerber
found the light, turned, and found her. He held her tightly
for a moment, just enjoying the feel of her body against
his. He kissed her throat, chin, and then lips. He reached
down, discovered the top button of her fatigue pants and
then laughed. "I just can't get used to feeling like this
about someone wearing a uniform.''

"I've never had a problem with it," said Karen. "I find
a uniform very sexy.''

Gerber finished with the buttons and let the pants drop.
He stepped back to look. The jungle jacket looked like a
short dress. "You look even better like that.''

She pulled him to her and kissed him. He kissed her
earlobe and held her. As he reached for the top button of
her jungle jacket, there was a knock on the door.

"Well, talk about timing.''

"Ignore it," said Karen.

There was another knock and then someone said, "Captain
Gerber? Are you in there?''

Gerber pulled Karen to the side so that she was behind
the door and whispered to her. "I've got to open it. It's
my team sergeant." He opened the door and peeked around
the corner.

"Sorry to bother you, Captain, but it looks like tonight.''

"You sure?''

"Not really, but all the indications are there. I think you
should come back with me.''

"You got an air asset?''

"Colonel Bates arranged it. It's army aviation. They're
not afraid of the dark. Well''—he laughed—"they might

be, but they'll never admit it, and they'll get us out there.''

"Okay, Fetterman. Meet me in the lobby in about five minutes. Bates knows I'm leaving?''

"Everything is cleared sir. The colonel said to tell you that General Crinshaw will flip out, but that he'll explain it so that you're free to come with me.''

"I'll see you in five.'' He closed the door and turned to Karen, "I'm sorry, darling, but I've got to go.''

She looked at him, the concern unmistakable in her eyes. "What's going on?''

"I really shouldn't tell you this, but it looks like Charlie is going to try to take my camp tonight.''

Karen felt her head swim. Her knees felt weak and the room began to spin. All she could say was "Oh my God.''

"I'll be all right.''

"Oh sure,'' she snapped. "You'll be fine with the whole VC army trying to overrun your camp. You'll be just fine.''

"I've got to go. You know that. You knew what I did that very first night. I never hid it from you.''

She pulled him close. "I know. I just didn't think it would be like this. I thought that . . . that somehow this wouldn't happen. It all seems so unreal. I mean . . .''

"I know what you mean,'' said Gerber quietly. "I won't tell you not to worry because I know you will. But I will say that you've given me a reason to survive. Just knowing that somebody cares whether I live or die somehow makes it easier. Makes me sure that I will live through this.''

"My God. You're talking like this is the end. That you're not coming back.''

"Karen, I will come back. I promise that.'' He stepped away, but took her hand, squeezing it. "I've got to go. I'm sorry about the evening.''

"Don't keep saying that. The evening doesn't matter. You just come back to me. That's all I want."

Gerber moved so that he could pick up his weapon. The .45 was still in his shoulder holster, hidden under his jungle jacket. He stared at Karen, trying to memorize what she looked like because he didn't have a picture. Then he leaned forward, kissed her lightly, and said, "No matter what happens, just remember one thing. I love you." Then he was gone.

Karen stared at the door, stunned. They had talked about a lot of different things, but never of love. It was like he was telling her this because he didn't expect to live through the night. At this thought, she gasped once and collapsed to the floor sobbing.

Gerber saw Fetterman standing by the lobby door. Outside he could see a jeep. Its engine was running. "How did you promote the jeep?"

"Colonel Bates did it. Said for us to hurry. It's beginning to look real grim out there. Charlie is massing on the other side of the border. Been up to it all day. I don't know if they've begun to move or not, but a forced march shouldn't hold them up that long. And we don't know how many people they've managed to infiltrate the last few days. It's really grim, Captain."

At the aircraft, Gerber was surprised to see Sergeant Krung and three of the Tai strikers sitting in the back of the helicopter waiting quietly.

"What's this?" he asked.

"Thought we might need some help. You can never tell, and a little extra help never hurts."

Gerber nodded and climbed aboard. Ten minutes later they were airborne.

CHAPTER 14 _____

Gerber leaned forward on the troop seat and tried to look out the cargo compartment door. Below him, the countryside was dark. Almost completely black. It wasn't like "the world," where there were hundreds of lights, from the farmer's security light, to the occasional gas station of chrome and neon, to small towns that were ablaze. Here light only made you a target, and even the candles and lanterns of the Vietnamese were extinguished early so that neither the VC nor the Americans would see them.

Far to the north there seemed to be something, but the light died quickly, as if it were a flare fired by someone who wanted to look at something hidden by the night. There was no follow-up. All Gerber could see was the dark of the ground, broken by ribbons of silver that were rivers, canals, and streams, and the black of the few roads.

He felt a tap on his shoulder and looked to see the crew chief holding out his flight helmet. The man leaned close so that he could shout into Gerber's ear. "Sir, the AC wants to talk to you. Put this on so you can hear him."

Gerber took the helmet, pushed the boom mike out of the way, and then studied the inside. There were black, rubberlike earphones, a couple of the tan pads, and a long black cord that came out the back and was plugged into the helicopter's intercom system.

165

"When you're ready to talk," shouted the crew chief, "you push this button."

Gerber took the small box that the crew chief held. Then he slipped the helmet over his head. He pushed the button and said, "What's happening?"

There was no response, and the crew chief pushed the boom mike up so that it was close to Gerber's lips. He nodded to indicate that it would work now.

"What's happening?" Gerber repeated.

The AC looked over his shoulder. He turned in the seat and said, "We're about twenty minutes from your camp. Your Lieutenant Bromhead has called to say that they have observed a buildup to the west of the camp and that they have been seeing movement all around, but so far they have taken no incoming rounds and have only seen the VC in the distance."

"He give you any idea how far out?"

"About a klick or so. Nobody is getting close yet."

"Numbers?"

"He said there was at least a battalion. He said that he thought there was more, but they hadn't spotted them yet. He said that we should approach the camp from the south."

Gerber repeated the information to Fetterman, who only nodded and said, "Hasn't changed much."

"Can you get a message through to Bromhead," Gerber asked the AC.

"Of course. You can talk to him youself, if you want. See that control just to your left?"

"Yes."

"When you're ready, just move the switch to position one."

Gerber moved to the control, twisted it and said, "Zulu Five, this is Zulu Six."

"Go ahead Six."

"Status?"

"Hasn't changed. We're picking up quite a bit of movement to the west and to the north. Still no incoming. I've laid on fast mover support through Stinger Ops. They're on call.''

"Good. You're doing fine. Keep me advised. I should be there in less than half an hour.''

"Roger. Zulu Five out.''

Gerber stripped the helmet and handed it back to the crew chief. He said, "They may call me again.''

The man nodded and held up a thumb to indicate he understood.

About twenty minutes later, they began a descent. The crew chief yelled that they were getting close and the AC thought that it was best that they approach low because they couldn't get enough altitude to stay out of the VC small-arms range.

Gerber nodded and checked the magazine of his M-14. He made sure that a round was chambered. He noticed that the door gunner was behind his weapon now and that it was loaded.

The crew chief shouted, "About five minutes.''

Then, from the right, Gerber heard a rattling, as the enemy on the ground opened fire. The door gunner swung his weapon around and began to shoot.

Gerber was staring at the floor in front of his feet, feeling helpless, when a hole exploded in it. And then another. He involuntarily tried to jump backward, but couldn't.

Fetterman calmly sat there. "Easy, Captain. We've been shot at before.''

"Yeah, but I don't want to go home with a bullet in the You know what that would look like.''

At that moment, Gerber was thrown to the left and back to the right. The engine noise suddenly increased, screaming almost as if it was in pain. There were three loud snaps, a grating shriek, and then silence. The crew chief yelled, "Brace yourself. We're going in.''

They hit the right skid, bounced to the left and back to

the right. The helicopter did not turn over, but came to rest, left side low, as if they had smashed the skid on that side. The door gunner was snapped back and forth, hitting his head against the bulkhead and momentarily stunning himself.

The AC popped his door and leaped out, running around to the other side so that he could check on the copilot.

Gerber unbuckled his seat belt, watched Fetterman do the same, and then got out. He ran ten or twelve yards out and dropped to the ground so that he could see where they were. Fetterman did the same on the opposite side of the downed aircraft. After sixty seconds, neither had seen anything move near them. Gerber crawled back, saw that Sergeant Krung and the other Tais were out, had their weapons ready, and were trying to cover the aircrewmen.

The AC moved close to Gerber and whispered. "We're not more than two klicks from the camp."

"The first thing we have to do," said Gerber, "is get away from here. The VC will be swarming all over in a couple of minutes."

"Then we have to destroy the aircraft. We can't leave it here for the Viet Cong."

"There's no way we can do that."

"Sure there is." The AC pointed to the spreading pool under the fuel cells. "Just toss a grenade under it and it should go up in two minutes."

"That would give our position away. There is no sense in providing Charlie with a beacon."

"But we can't leave it."

"Captain," said Fetterman, "we had better move out."

"Do you have a smoke grenade?" Gerber asked the AC.

The crew chief handed him one. Gerber pulled the pin and tossed it away. He knelt near the ruptured fuel tanks and then looked up. "Give me the ammo can. Take out all but two, three hundred rounds."

The crew chief did so and handed it down. Gerber set it

on the ground, dug a small hole out from under it, and placed the grenade in it so that the safety lever was held in place by the can. Gerber said, "Charlie won't be able to resist this. He'll pick up the can and release the safety lever. The grenade will go off immediately since they don't have delay fuses in smoke grenades, and the flame under it will set off the fuel."

The AC smiled. "Great!"

Fetterman stepped close. "We're ready. Krung has the point. I figure that I should bring up the rear. We can keep the aircrew in the center for protection."

"Let's go."

Instead of moving directly toward the camp, they moved nearly due west, angling for the riverbank. If, for some reason, they couldn't get to the camp, they could probably find refuge along the river.

They walked quietly, slowly, each man being careful so that he didn't make noise. While the Tais seemed to be at home in the jungle, able to glide through it, missing the things that would make noise, and the Green Berets knew enough about it to keep silent, the aircrewmen were having trouble. They stumbled, bumped into bushes, and rattled equipment. Fetterman kept falling back, trying to separate himself from the aircrew by enough distance so he could avoid any hastily prepared ambush, triggered by the aircrew's water-buffalo approach to noise discipline, but would be able to lend assistance.

But Krung had stopped. Gerber moved forward and found the Tai sergeant crouching under a large bush, watching three men working to set up a mortar tube. Krung heard Gerber approach and motioned him down. He put his lips next to Gerber's ear and told him what he saw.

Gerber looked back, saw that Fetterman was working his way close. When he got down, Gerber said, "We can't move. We can't fire because we don't know how many of them there are."

"The lieutenant knows we're down, doesn't he?"

"I would think so. But I hope he has the good sense to keep everyone inside the camp. They can't help us now."

Just at that moment, the VC dropped a round into the tube. Gerber ducked, but Fetterman kept his eyes on the enemy. Within a couple of minutes, mortar tubes that were now surrounding the camp began firing. Some of the Vietnamese in the camp tried to return fire with their rifles. They probably wouldn't have much luck, but they were making a lot of noise.

"We can use the firing to cover us and take out the mortar crew," said Gerber. "I'll cover you and Krung and one of the Tais while you move in with your knives."

"If I might suggest, Captain," said Fetterman. "I've got my M-3. It's fairly quiet. Maybe I should cover."

Gerber looked at the silenced weapon cradled in Fetterman's arms. "Okay. I'll pass the word. You find a place where you can watch."

While Fetterman moved backward, and began working his way to a place to cover the attack, Gerber slid to the right. He pulled his knife and showed it to Krung. Then he pointed to the VC using the mortar, gesturing with the knife. Krung understood immediately. He tapped the shoulder of the Tai next to him and went through the same sign language that Gerber had used. The man nodded his understanding.

As the VC fired a round, Gerber nodded and the three of them slipped out of the jungle and into the tiny clearing the VC were using. In a low crouch, they moved forward. The VC all had their backs to the attackers.

Just as Gerber reached his man, the one to the right who was holding a mortar round, turned and saw them. Gerber could do nothing other than grab his man under the chin and lift so that he could slice the throat.

Krung had attacked his man, killing him with the knife quickly by puncturing the man's kidney and pushing the knife upward, trying to hit the lungs and heart. The man died before he knew what was happening.

The third man stood rooted for a moment, watching his comrades die. But as the Tai moved in for the kill, the VC threw the mortar round at him. It struck him in the head, and the Tai went down, reaching up.

Before the VC could move, there was a muffled burp and the VC pitched forward on his face. He started to get up and then collapsed into the dirt. Gerber leaped to the man, tossed his rifle, which was still slung on the enemy's shoulder, away, and then checked to see if he was dead.

There was a noise at the very edge of the clearing and Gerber spun toward it, leveling his now unslung rifle. The AC and the pilot both stepped out. Gerber growled at them, "Get down." He turned and saw Krung taking his trophy, and said, "We don't have time for that." He was annoyed, not because Krung was taking the dead man's genitals, but because he thought they didn't have time to fulfill personal vendettas.

While the Tais worked at policing up the tube and collecting the enemy weapons, Gerber stepped to the pilots. "You guys have to be careful. You can't go walking around out here like its a stroll through the park."

"But the enemy has been killed."

"Just the ones you can see. You don't know if they were all killed. There could have been others. And you don't know where all our people are. You could have screwed up the people who were covering us."

The copilot was going to protest further, but the AC cut him off saying, "Sorry. I didn't think."

Gerber left them to find Fetterman. He said, "Let's move toward the camp. I wish there was a way we could talk to them. You should have brought a radio."

Fetterman stared at him for an instant and then said, "Yes sir. Didn't anticipate being shot down."

"I have a radio."

They both turned to look at the AC. Gerber said, "Why didn't you say something before now."

"It's just a survival radio. Only good on two-forty-three decimal zero."

"But we monitor that frequency." Gerber held out his hand and said, "How's it work?"

The AC pulled on the antenna, handed it over, and, pointing to a button on the side, said, "The antenna activates it. Just push the button and talk."

Gerber whispered, "Zulu Five, this is Zulu Six." He waited for a moment and repeated the message.

The response came quickly, and loudly. "Zulu Six, this is Zulu Five."

"Jesus," said Gerber.

The AC reached over and turned down the volume. "Sorry."

Gerber keyed the radio. "Five, we are down and safe. We are approximately one klick out, near point Hotel Lima." Gerber couldn't be more exact because he hadn't brought a grid map with him. He tried to remember the landmarks on the maps that he and Bromhead had devised so they could give each other coordinates over the radio and any enemy listening wouldn't be able to understand.

"Roger. Say instructions."

"We're going to try to join you. Will make contact when in position. Can you advise about enemy troop placements?"

"Major concentrations to your two o'clock and seven o'clock. We have observed activity in your area and believe there might be a mortar position situated in that general location."

"Roger." Gerber wanted to tell Bromhead that they had eliminated the mortar, but was afraid that it would provide too much information to anyone who might be monitoring.

"Do you want me to send a patrol out?"

"Negative. You're going to need everyone you have. We'll get there ourselves. If we get into trouble, we'll shout." He didn't want to say anything more, so he pushed the antenna in, shutting off the radio.

He turned to Krung, pointed toward the camp and motioned him forward. They spread out again, Krung leading, one of the Tais behind him, and the one who had been hit by the thrown mortar round walking with the flight crew. The man had only been momentarily stunned, but now complained of double vision.

From around the area, there was the continual pop of the mortars and the sustained fire from various camp machine guns. They were directed, more or less, at the enemy mortar tubes, but weren't having much effect. What worried Gerber the most was that Bromhead would launch a series of flares. As of now, the attack was mainly a mortar duel, and the camp's mortars were dropping rounds as close to the enemy positions as they could. The machine guns were for Vietnamese morale since they probably wouldn't hit anything at that range. Flares would be needed if any kind of advance was made on the camp, but they would show Gerber and his party as well as the enemy. Everyone would be able to see everyone else.

If they could run, or even walk at a normal pace, they could be in camp in fifteen minutes or less. But they had to be quiet and keep to cover. With the enemy all around them and the trigger-happy Vietnamese on the walls of the camp, they had to be careful.

They had gotten close when Krung signaled them to get down. Gerber crawled to him and looked. In front of them was what looked like a staging area for one of the enemy units. Gerber tapped Krung and nodded to the rear.

When they were clear, Krung demanded, "Why leave? Many Cong. We kill."

"We kill. But not now."

With the rest of the men, Gerber led them away from the VC. As soon as they had taken cover, he got out the radio. He whispered, "Zulu Five, this is Six. I have a target. Range three hundred meters. At point Hotel Hotel. Give me one round of WP."

Bromhead had the good sense not to answer until he could say, "Shot, over."

"Shot out." Gerber waited, saw the round drop to the right of the enemy and about fifty meters short. He gave the information to Bromhead. With the correction, the next round dropped into the middle of the VC. Gerber said, "On target. Fire for effect."

There was a rapid series of explosions, walking around the VC formation. After several minutes, Bromhead came on the radio and said, "Last rounds on the way."

When they detonated, Bromhead asked, "Can you check the damage?"

"Affirmative." Gerber shut off the radio, told Krung, and they started off again. They found what remained of the VC unit. Gerber counted thirty bodies. That done, they circled the area so that they could proceed to the camp.

They weren't more than a hundred and fifty meters from the outer wire. Gerber had turned to the AC to tell him that they were going to have to wait a moment when there was a shot. Everyone fell to the ground. There was a second shot and then a burst of machine gun fire. Gerber tried to see who was shooting, knowing from the sharp cracks of the weapon that it was an AK and not an American rifle.

He rolled to his side, saw that the flight crew was all right. Then, out of the dark loomed two shapes. Gerber swung his rifle and pulled the trigger just as one of the Tais did. Both the shapes fell, but there were a dozen bursts from automatic weapons, kicking up dirt all around them.

Gerber scrambled to his left. He slipped the selector on his M-14 to full automatic. Behind him, he heard the strange muffled snap of Fetterman's silenced M-3 and then a groan. To his left was the crack of a pistol. Suddenly, all around, nearly everyone was shooting. Both pilots were using their pistols, and the crew chief and door gunner were firing M-14s.

The firing around him increased in volume. It was clear

that more VC were joining the firefight and that there were so many of them around that Gerber and his tiny group would soon be overrun. He pulled out the radio and called Bromhead to advise him. He ended saying, "You'll be dropping the rounds almost on top of us, but it's our only hope."

He waited for thirty seconds, but nothing happened. There was shooting all around him. The noise was becoming a steady roar, and for one irrational moment Gerber thought that he had lied to Karen. He wasn't going to be all right.

The radio crackled to life. Bromhead said, "There is a patrol en route your location."

"Negative. Use the mortars."

"The patrol has already cleared the wire. Warn your people."

Gerber knew that it was useless to argue now. He could ream Bromhead royally, if they both survived the night. Now he had to warn the others so they wouldn't accidentally shoot their own rescue party.

A flare burst overhead, catching nearly everyone by surprise. Gerber wondered if Bromhead had fired it, but decided that the young lieutenant wouldn't make that mistake. It had to be something done by the VC.

In the half-light of the dying flare, Gerber could see nearly fifty VC surrounding them. He opened fire, single-shot, picking his targets so that each round counted. He watched five of the enemy fall from his fire before the flare went out.

When it was dark, Gerber tried to consolidate his tiny perimeter, pulling Krung back to join them. Fetterman moved into the perimeter without being told, firing his silenced M-3.

Suddenly, to the north of them, near the wire, there was a wild burst of firing, a sustained yell in Vietnamese, and then a dozen VC ran into the center of his perimeter. Gerber and Fetterman crouched to meet them, but they weren't interested in fighting. They had dropped their weapons and were fleeing. Both Gerber and Fetterman fired at the running VC.

From the other direction came the unmistakable voice of Lieutenant Minh. In his strange, clipped English, he shouted, "We're here, old boy."

Gerber ran forward, saw the Vietnamese lieutenant, and then the twenty men he had brought with him. Gerber didn't wait, he grabbed the arm of one of the aircrewmen and pushed him toward the rescue party. To the others, he said, "Come on. Let's go."

Minh didn't wait for any orders from Gerber. He started his patrol back to the camp. The point men, two of his most trusted NCOs, ran ahead. One of them fired a burst from his Thompson submachine gun, killing a VC that had gotten between them and the camp.

Fetterman didn't need orders either. He moved backward, to take a position as the rear guard. Gerber tried to get the flight crew to their feet so that he could move them out.

Minh and the Vietnamese didn't hang around. As soon as they had eliminated the opposition and broken through to the trapped Americans, they started back to the camp.

Three VC leaped out of the dark, grabbing at the Vietnamese, killing two of them. Minh whirled, clubbing a VC in the head with his rifle butt. The remaining two tried to escape, but were bayoneted by the Vietnamese. Minh had lost two men.

They reached the outer wire. A mortar round dropped next to them. One man was killed and two more were injured. From the camp, there came an almost unbroken burst of firing. Gerber dragged out the radio and almost shouted. "Five. Hold your fire. You have us pinned down in the wire."

For another couple of seconds it continued, gradually tapering off as the Americans in the camp kicked and clawed at the Vietnamese, trying to tell them that their own people were going to be killed.

Two more mortar rounds dropped close to them. After the second explosion, Minh leaped to his feet and almost sprinted through the wire toward the gate. His men, some of them reluctantly, followed. Gerber and the others did the same, spreading out so that a couple of yards separated them all.

It didn't take them long to get inside the camp. Most immediately fell to the ground, taking cover so that they would have time to catch their breaths.

Gerber got down to one knee, breathed deeply, and then said to Fetterman, "Get the aircrewmen to the command bunker. Have Minh get his people back on the wall and then join me at the fire control tower."

"Yes sir."

Gerber got up, heard the distant pop of a mortar firing, and dived for cover. When he heard the round hit, he got to his feet, ran to the fire control tower, and looked up. He slowly became aware of all the shooting going on around him. Mortars and grenades were exploding, most of them in the distance. He heard machine guns and rifles and occasionally the whirring of a round that passed close.

There was nothing to do at the base of the tower. He had to get up there, to survey the area and get a full report from Bromhead. He slung his rifle, grabbed the bottom rung, and nearly ran up the ladder. At the top, he leaped over the sandbags, landing head-first in the tower.

Bromhead looked down at him and said, "Welcome home, Captain."

"Thanks. How's it look?"

Unaware that he was echoing the words of Sergeant Fetterman, he said, "Grim, Captain. Really grim."

CHAPTER 15 _____

"Don't try to be melodramatic," said Gerber, "just tell me how bad it is."

"Like I said, 'Grim.' Bocker and Kepler ran recon patrols last night and this morning. They came in after you left for Saigon. Lots and lots of activity, especially around Moc Phoc. Derek says they're building lots of coffins and ladders in the village."

"How many is lots?"

"Christ, Captain, I don't know. Derek said he counted sixty, seventy coffins, and over a hundred ladders, and that's just in Moc Phoc."

"I think I liked it better when you were melodramatic."

"Not only that, but Bocker says there's been heavy traffic all along both sides of the river since midafternoon. He figures four, maybe five battalions. And Bocker isn't one to exaggerate. After I got that cheery news I thought I had better send Fetterman to collect you."

"██████, five battalions. Are you sure?"

"No sir. Could be more. Like seven or eight. Bocker only counted enough for five battalions. Course they'll be a platoon less of them now."

"Great. That only leaves one thousand seven hundred and ten VC to go. That we know of."

Both men ducked as a burst of heavy machine gun rounds raked the fire control tower.

"Twelve-sevens out near the river," said Bromhead. "They're getting better. That's the first time they've hit the tower."

"And it's going to be their last. We're going to stop this shit right now. Kittredge, get some mortars on those guys."

"Right." Kittredge peeked cautiously over the sandbags, then took a sighting on the incoming tracers with the range finder, and phoned the information down to the 81mm pits.

Gerber turned to Bromhead. "We got any patrols or LPs still out?"

"Negative. I pulled everyone in about an hour ago."

"Okay, I want you to get over to the forward bunker on the west wall and take direct command of defenses there. By the way, where's Captain Trang?"

"In the command bunker. I believe he's taken charge of the sandbags and telephone."

"Great. He can keep the helicopter pilots company. You better get going, Johnny."

As Bromhead started to climb over the sandbags, he was almost knocked back onto the platform by Fetterman.

"Christ, sir. Stay out of the way."

Bromhead didn't answer. He slipped back over the sandbags and dropped down the ladder, sprinting across the pockmarked runway.

At that moment the attack began in earnest, and Bromhead vanished behind a solid wall of flame as a salvo of 240mm rockets slammed into the command bunker, killing Captain Trang, Sergeants Hinh and Lim, and the entire helicopter crew. Sergeant Kittredge was flung bodily out of the fire control tower by the force of the explosion almost immediately under it. The tower stood upright for nearly two full seconds before slowly toppling over on its side like a mortally wounded ox.

Stunned, Gerber sat up, looked around, and was horrified to see Kittredge's arm sticking from beneath a large pile of ruptured sandbags. He scrambled forward and began tossing sandbags off the heavy-weapons sergeant.

Fetterman, blood streaming down his face, heaved a timber off his own leg, then crawled forward to help. "Is he dead?"

"I don't think so. At least he's breathing. Can you get him to the doc? I've got to get over to the commo bunker."

"Help me get him up." Fetterman threw Kittredge over his shoulder in a fireman's carry and ran for the infirmary.

Dazed, Gerber glanced around and found his rifle. The barrel was bent at a forty-five-degree angle. He pulled the magazine out of the weapon and tossed the rifle away. Kicking aside a sandbag, he retrieved Kittredge's rifle, made sure it would operate, and ran for the commo bunker. Amid the sounds of battle, the air was filled with bugles.

Bromhead painfully sucked air into his lungs and pushed himself up off the runway. His head hurt and it felt like something kept sticking him in the back. He looked around for his rifle but couldn't find it. He drew his .45 and started for the west wall.

Of the camp's officers, only Minh on the south wall had any idea of what was going on. Seconds after the shattering rocket barrage had struck the camp, splintering the timbers of the fire control tower and destroying the command bunker, the Viet Cong infantry had attacked en masse.

Minh gave the order for the riflemen lining the wall to commence firing. The machine guns and recoilless rifles were already putting out rounds. Minh grabbed up the handset of the Lima Lima and tried to call the fire control tower. When he got no answer, he tried the command bunker. That failing, he tried the commo bunker and found Sergeant Bocker.

"I say, old boy, I can't seem to raise anyone up in the tower or at the command bunker."

"Blown up. Both of them."

"Connect me with 60mm pit one, pit two, and pit three."

"All at once?"

"If that's quite convenient. Otherwise, the south end of the camp is about to be overrun. Do hurry. Those chaps are in the wire."

Quickly Minh fed estimated range and direction information to the mortar crews and adjusted their fire until it was dropping directly on the front ranks of the VC. Then he had Bocker patch him through to the 81mm pits for illumination.

In addition to the 81mm, trip flares were going up. Red and green tracers were crisscrossing. Sully Smith's mines, their red and white flashes marking them as they detonated, were punching holes in the incoming enemy.

Even with the added firepower from the 60mm mortars, the VC didn't waver, clearing the second strand of wire. Minh reached around and pulled his bayonet from the scabbard, clipping it underneath the barrel of his rifle.

"Company will prepare to fix bayonets," he shouted. "Fix *bayonets*!"

The VC had reached the last strand of concertina.

On the west wall, Bromhead stared in disbelief as nearly two full companies of Viet Cong rushed his position. They were already through the second strand of wire. "Oh Christ," he said. "This is where I came in."

Bromhead grabbed the handset of the field phone and tried to raise the 60mm mortar pits, telling them that he needed support immediately.

"But sir, Lieutenant Minh has just ordered us to fire in support of the south wall."

"We're about to be overrun here."

"So is he."

Bromhead slammed the phone down and cocked his pistol. "Prepare to fix bayonets," he shouted. "Fix *bayonets*!"

*   *   *

At the commo bunker, Gerber said, "Well, shit. What else could go wrong."

Then he found out.

Gerber had taken a PRC-10 and a field phone to the top of the commo bunker, the highest remaining point in camp. From there he could observe the enemy movements. In the south, he saw a strong enemy force about to overrun Minh. In the west he saw another large force about to overrun Bromhead. And then, in the east, he saw a fresh VC battalion forming for an assault across the paddies. Gerber hadn't believed that the VC would attempt an assault across so much open ground. The plan seemed foolhardy. But with the defenses breaking down in the south and west, it no longer seemed so laughable.

He picked up the handset on the field phone. "Galvin, you better alert Stinger Ops. We're going to need the fast movers and a flare ship, and if they could have gotten them here an hour ago, it would have almost been too late. I'll be heading for the east wall and I'll take the PRC-10 with me."

Having finished, he tossed the handset away, grabbed the radio, and climbed to the ground. He raced to the central bunker on the east wall and found Sully Smith inside.

"Good evening, Captain. Glad to see you."

"What's the story here?"

"Well, it's quite simple, sir. We got about ten more rounds for the recoilless, no rounds for the fifty, and we can't get mortar support because Minh has them all tied up. That leaves us with about five hundred rounds for the .30-cal. Other than that we're in deep shit."

"So what's the bad news?"

"I figure there are about five hundred VC about to hit us."

"Sully, you have a talent for understatement."

"But we have one round left for each of the VC."

"What about mines?"

"Already used those."

Gerber stood silent for moment and then said, "Well, shit, I suppose there's only one thing to do."

"What's that, Captain?"

"Fix bayonets."

"Before you do that, Captain, I think there's one little thing you ought to know."

On the north wall, Lieutenant Bao turned to Sergeant Tyme. "We go help Lieutenant Johnny now?"

Tyme carefully studied the empty ground in front of the wall. "Leave the people in the bunkers. We'll take all the people off the wall and have them fix bayonets. Then we go help Lieutenant Johnny now."

The VC had breached the last strand of concertina and thrown their ladders across the pungi moat. They had scrambled up the earthen embankment and engaged the defenders.

By this time, Bromhead had emptied his pistol, reloaded, and emptied it again, finally hurling it into the face of a VC soldier who was trying to bayonet him. Bromhead picked up the rifle and impaled the man with his own weapon. The bayonet caught in the man's ribs, and Bromhead pulled the trigger, letting the recoil jerk the blade free.

Bromhead turned to meet another threat. As the man thrust at him, Bromhead parried, sidestepped, and kicked the man in the groin. As the VC doubled over in pain, Bromhead slashed him across the throat.

It was then that the central bunker exploded. VC sappers had finally gotten close enough to toss a satchel charge into it. With the loss of the recoilless rifle and the two automatic weapons in the bunker, the defenders could no longer hold their position on the wall and were slowly pushed back.

Bromhead, realizing that the loss of the west wall would mean the loss of the entire camp, tried desperately to find some inner defensive position where he could rally the remainder of his troops. There was none. The only possibility for an inner defense was with the bunker complex on the opposite side of the runway, and they could not retreat to that point without exposing the backs of the men on the south wall. Bromhead pulled his men into a tight group and gave ground slowly.

The VC leaped over the wall.

Out of the frying pan and into the fire.

With the roar of a demon from hell itself, a solid wall of flame spread across the earthen embankment, engulfing men in fiery death. Flamethrower in hand, Sergeant Fetterman had arrived.

The attack broke and the VC fled, allowing Bromhead to retake the wall.

"Mortar crew said you needed some illumination, sir. How's that?"

"~~Goddamn~~ near perfect," Bromhead said, happily. "I could ~~damn~~ near kiss your ugly face, Sergeant."

"If you do, I'll take my flamethrower and go home."

"Take me with you if you do."

On the other side of the wall, reinforced by a fresh company, the VC officers rallied their men.

Sergeants Kepler and Clarke hadn't been directly involved in the fighting. They had been on the east corner of the north wall, in a bunker with two .30-cal. machine guns. Later they had moved to the 81mm pits to help provide illumination when it was called for, but the Vietnamese and Tai crews had been well trained and were capable of handling the job. Both sergeants felt useless. When Lieutenant Minh asked for illumination and mortar support, saying that he was about to be overrun, they decided that they were needed on the south wall.

But they also knew that they would be running low on

ammunition there. Gerber had said that they would find
that a major problem would be getting ammo from the
rearm bunker to the positions on the wall. Since they
didn't know where the main assault would be directed,
they tried to locate the bunker so that it was equidistant
from the central bunker on each wall.

Kepler stood outside, while Clarke ran in. He found a
.30-cal. machine gun that they hadn't had time to place. He
grabbed it and several boxes of ammo. He handed those
out the door to Kepler, and disappeared back inside. He
found more ammo, picked up as much as he could carry,
and ran out.

They started off, running along the side of the runway.
They found a half-dozen Vietnamese crouching behind a
stack of sandbags that hadn't been used. Clarke screamed
at them, partly so he could be heard over the noise of the
battle and partly because he couldn't believe they were just
sitting around. He handed the ammo he carried to them,
and told Kepler to go because he wanted to take three of
them back to the rearm bunker for more ammo.

Kepler took two steps and discovered another small
group of Vietnamese. The NCO with them had been
wounded, taking shrapnel in the shoulder. He wasn't sure
what he should do. Kepler told him to follow along.

There was a third group clustered near the burning
remains of the framework for the civilian bunker. Kepler
was glad that they hadn't gotten most of the Vietnamese
families moved to the camp yet. He now had nineteen men
with him.

They rounded the corner of a half-completed hootch
near the south end of the runway and came face-to-face
with a group of VC sappers. Kepler dropped the unloaded
.30-cal. machine gun, but before he could unsling his rifle,
one of the VC rushed him, head down, bayonet extended.
Kepler swung the ammo can he held in his left hand
upward, hitting the barrel of the enemy's rifle. He then
brought the can down, with as much force as he could

muster, crushing the man's skull. He dropped the bloody ammo can and, ignoring his rifle, drew his pistol.

Next to him, the wounded NCO had stepped forward to meet the thrust of another Viet Cong. With his own rifle, he pushed the enemy's to the side and then pulled the trigger. The VC took three rounds in the stomach.

Kepler stepped back, turning to the left so that he could meet the threat there. He shot three of the VC, clubbed a fourth, and turned to the right. He watched the NCO smash the butt of his rifle into the face of an enemy, continue the motion so that he could bayonet the VC next to him.

Firing erupted around him as both sides gave up on close hand-to-hand and tried to shoot each other. Kepler was afraid of accidently shooting their own men on the south wall, but they couldn't leave the sappers free to roam.

He dropped to one knee, firing only when he had a sure target.

Behind him, someone shouted *"Grenade!"*

Kepler flattened on the ground as the Vietnamese with him did the same. There was a series of explosions, and then the voice said, "Kill them."

Kepler was up, rushing the sappers, shooting those who moved. Clarke ran up behind him with the three men he had taken to the rearm point.

Clarke said, simply, "Looked like you could use some help."

"Right."

Quickly, they picked up the enemy weapons and explosives so that any VC left alive, who might revive, would be no real threat to anyone.

With the remaining men—six had been killed in the brief fight—Kepler and Clarke ran for the south wall. Minh had temporarily fought the VC to a standstill. Kepler came up and said, "Where do you want us, Lieutenant?"

Minh looked back over his shoulder. "I'm not sure, old boy. Could use a spot of assistance on the east side."

Kepler could see that the bunker anchoring that corner had been nearly destroyed, probably by a satchel charge. He nodded his understanding.

Just as they began to move, firing increased along the wall and there was a surging charge through the gaps blown in the wire. Minh shouted something in Vietnamese and turned to Kepler and Clarke. "Here they come again."

Without a word, Kepler turned and ran, Clarke and some of the Vietnamese right behind him. He dropped his .30-cal. and extra ammo near the remains of the bunker and began tossing sandbags toward the earth embankment.

The VC were steering away from that corner of the base. They were trying to force their way through the center, near the one gate, so that they would be able to overrun the airstrip. That way they could attack all the camp defenders from behind.

Kepler and Clarke finished building their makeshift wall, set up the machine gun, and while Clarke fed the weapon, Kepler raked the VC near the first strand of concertina, trying to halt the flow of enemy reinforcements.

When the machine gun began firing, two dozen Viet Cong, realizing the threat, changed directions, running straight for Kepler and Clarke. The wounded Vietnamese NCO leaped to the wall, shouted, and then toppled over as he was shot again and again. Those men who had been with him jumped to the wall and ran forward to engage the VC. It was as if they were enraged by the death of their sergeant.

They waded in, swinging their rifles and using their bayonets. There was some shooting, but very little because the men were too close together. But there were just too many VC, and even though a couple of the defenders tried to get back to the wall, they were all killed.

As soon as they were all down, Kepler opened fire again, shooting as many of the VC as he could. Once that threat was eliminated, he began trying to break the assault near Minh. Clarke tossed grenades when he was able.

Even with that, the VC reached the earthen embankment again and clawed their way up it. Minh, leading his men, leaped up to meet the enemy. With bayonet and knife, they fought to keep the VC out of the camp.

Minh was screaming, the words unintelligible, lost in the sound of the hammering machine guns, the bursting of grenades and mortars, the cries of the wounded and dying. Fifty or sixty of the defenders were yelling for the medics, but the medics were too busy to help much. They were wading through blood and gore almost too deep to believe.

Another group of VC slipped along the wall, just staying out of the pungi filled moat, but using some of the earthen embankment for cover. With the defenders all engaged in preventing the enemy from penetrating the wall, the VC thought they could slip over it and get behind the defenders.

They popped up near Kepler and Clarke, swarming over the wall and dropping between the two Green Berets. Clarke whipped his rifle around, shooting a half-dozen enemy before emptying his magazine. With bayonet, he slashed and thrust, killing two more of the enemy.

Kepler picked up the machine gun, swinging it so that he could shoot the VC as they reached the top of the wall, but the belt broke. He then began using the weapon as a club.

There was a sudden pain in his back, and he jerked forward, away from it. He turned, saw a VC soldier with a bayonet, and threw the .30-cal. at him. His rifle had been lying on the ground near him, but in the confusion, he couldn't see it. He pulled his pistol, shot the man, then two others, who rushed him, and dropped to his knees. He found one of the AKs, picked it up, stabbed an enemy close to him, and turned in time to see three VC converge on Clarke.

Kepler bayoneted one of them, knocked the second to the ground, and watched as Clarke clubbed the third.

Clarke spun to cover the downed VC. Kepler turned to look, but the attack broke, the VC fleeing through the wire back toward the river. They didn't stop until they were out of small-arms range.

Both Kepler and Clarke stared into the quiet dark. It was only quiet on the south wall. Around them, they could hear shooting, but the volume had decreased. Near them they could hear the moans of the wounded.

Kepler looked at Clarke, saw the arm of his uniform was tattered and covered with blood. He said, "Here, let me help you," but slipped to the ground, suddenly weak from blood loss from the wound on his lower back. Clarke tried to patch him up. He could tell that Kepler wasn't fatally wounded. Once he had taken care of Kepler, he moved on to help as many of the other wounded as possible. He didn't waste time on those who would die soon because he couldn't help them anyway.

Unlike the movies, there were no really clean wounds. There were missing limbs and gaping holes that dangled intestines and poured pools of blood. If he hadn't been so busy, Clarke might have been sick. He didn't have the time.

Bromhead pushed his way to the wall. Bodies, both defender and VC, littered the ground on either side of it. For a moment Bromhead thought that they had inflicted enough casualties to break the assault. Then he saw a fresh VC company racing across the open ground to join those men who were just on the other side of the wall.

There was a bugle call, another, and then a dozen. The VC surged forward, crossed the pungi moat easily on their ladders, and began the rush over the last few yards. Fetterman popped up and used his flamethrower again. Nearly all the VC started to shoot at him. He dropped down, out of sight, while the defenders fired at the enemy.

When the incoming fire tapered off, Fetterman jumped up and used the flamethrower a final time. He caused enough confusion for the attack to falter a moment. But then he ran out of fuel, and when the flamethrower sputtered out, the VC rallied, dashed up the embankment, and engaged the defenders.

There were too many of the enemy, and the VC flooded around Bromhead and his men. Now he didn't even have the option to fall back. They were surrounded, and fighting for their lives. Slowly the VC were killing the defenders, taking the wall and bunkers.

Bromhead, using the rifle he had found, stood nearly back to back with Fetterman, who had shrugged out of the flamethrower, using the heavy tanks to smash the skulls of the two VC before discarding it. Together, they managed to keep the Viet Cong away from each other, killing those who got too close to them.

Bromhead knew they couldn't hold out much longer. He had a sinking feeling in his stomach, not because he thought he was about to die, but because he had failed. All he had to do was keep the VC from taking the wall, and he hadn't been able to do it. Now the whole camp would be lost.

But even if he failed, Bromhead was determined to make the enemy success as costly as possible. He kept the VC dead piling up.

From the north, he heard a roar and turned to see Lieutenant Bao and Sergeant Tyme leading nearly seventy Tais. There was little shooting until they reached the wall. Then there was a lot. The VC, caught by surprise a second time, gave ground slowly for a moment and then broke. It was a rout.

This time, the VC officers couldn't contain them. They fell back, across the moat and through the wire, until they disappeared from sight.

Bromhead turned and saw Bao and Tyme. "Talk about just in time. I don't think we could have held on much longer."

"We come to help, Lieutenant Johnny."

"You did just fine." Bromhead smiled at Bao.

In the distance, they heard the plop of mortars being fired, and Fetterman yelled, "Incoming."

Bromhead and Fetterman thought there would be another attack. They didn't know that the VC were withdrawing slowly, leaving only enough men to draw fire and create a diversion. The battle plan had been changed.

It was on the east wall that the decisive fight would take place. Gerber and Smith stood in the central bunker, studying the enemy, who still hadn't moved. The size of the force opposing them seemed to be growing.

Gerber realized that he wasn't hearing much from the mortar pits. Both Bromhead and Minh had forgotten about the mortars when the fighting had turned hand-to-hand. And with the enemy mixed in with their own men, they couldn't use the mortars effectively.

Gerber picked up the field phone and told Bocker to give him the 60mm mortar pits. He fed them the range, direction, and charge so they could begin dropping HE on the enemy. He then told the 81mm pits to give him illumination.

When the first of the illumination rounds burst overhead, the Vietnamese on the wall began shooting. It was sporadic and not well aimed.

On the field phone, Gerber said, "Where's the fast movers?"

"Stinger Ops has said that they have scrambled the aircraft. They should be on the way."

"Flare ship?"

"Same thing, Captain. On the way."

"Keep me informed."

Still the enemy didn't move. They stayed where they were, the assault force growing. Mortars began dropping among them, scattering some. Then bugle calls filled the air and the black-clad horde began the rush across the paddies.

Unnecessarily, Gerber yelled, "Fire. Fire!"

The heavy weapons had been sited so that they would channel any attacking force onto specific paths. The mines were laid to complement the heavy weapons.

But none were left.

"You better get your last surprise ready, Sully. I think they've sent the entire army this time."

The VC came on, the mortars walking with them but not causing many casualties. The intensity of fire from the wall increased, but was still ineffective.

Near him, Gerber heard the .30-caliber open fire, the rapid hammering adding to the confusion. To Smith, he said, "Whenever, Sully."

Smith picked up another of his jury-rigged control panels. Holding it in one hand, he leaned forward so that he could see out the firing slit of the bunker, trying to keep his ear away from the hammering .30-cal. Under his breath, he mumbled, "Come on. Come on. You're almost there."

Out in the rice paddies, Smith could see the one white rock that he had set out to mark the paddy he had doctored. He saw a dozen men pass it, and saw that there were fifty or sixty behind them. Smith threw the switch on his control.

The camp's generator cut in, the three-phase lead electrifying the water in the paddy. The VC caught in the water didn't know what hit them. They jerked and spasmed as the electricity, conducted by the water, flowed through them. Before they realized what was happening, several other VC jumped into the paddy to help and were caught. Smith opened the switch, and the men, the few still standing in the paddy, fell into the water. Now the VC gave that area a wide berth. They didn't know what had happened, but they wanted to make sure that it didn't happen to them. Nearly fifty had died.

There was confusion around that one paddy. But it did nothing to hold up the attack. Where the concertina was still intact, the VC threw themselves on it, letting those behind them leap over it. But there were so many holes in it already that not many had to do that.

Firing along the wall became more accurate as the targets got closer. Gaps appeared in the human wave rushing forward, but they were filled quickly. Gerber had thought that the enemy was throwing a battalion at him, but it was closer to two.

In one hand, he still held the handset of the field phone. He was talking to all the mortar pits, adjusting their fire as the enemy came closer. The rain of mortar shells was taking a heavy toll now, but the VC ignored it, reaching the pungi moat that was the final barrier.

But with all the mortars and Smith's trick, the VC had somehow lost most of the ladders that would have been used to cross the moat. Three or four of them tried to jump, but the moat was too wide, and they fell among the sharpened bamboo stakes.

Gerber had an inspiration. He ordered the mortars to momentarily cease fire. Without that behind them, the VC started to fall back, slowly at first, and then faster. The attack broke before the VC even reached the wall.

And the battalion, that had been fresh, had been badly mauled. For a moment, Gerber thought that they had beaten them so badly that they wouldn't be able to mount another assault.

He turned back to the firing port and said, "Sully, that was a good gag. Worked like a dream."

"Yes sir. Too bad they'll stay out of that paddy now."

"Doesn't matter." On the field phone he said, "Bocker, where the hell are the faster movers?"

"ETA of twenty minutes, Captain."

"Twenty minutes? What's the problem?"

"I don't know, sir. They said it would be twenty minutes."

Then, from the other side of the bunker, he heard Smith say, "Oh my God."

Gerber looked out the firing slit. Facing them was what

looked like another full battalion. Not the remains of the one they had faced, but a whole new one.

Gerber almost echoed Smith's words. "My God, I hope that's the last one they have."

With no kind of warning, the VC started forward, bugles mixing with their shouts. The firing picked up again as the defenders tried to break the assault. But this time there were too many VC, there were no tricks left, and they had all their ladders.

Gerber called for the mortars.

There was only a moment's hesitation at the pungi moat. The VC leaped up on the ladders, balancing precariously over the stakes. The defenders shot many of them, but more were always there, ready to move forward. The Viet Cong gained a foothold, regrouped, and began trying to climb the dirt wall.

In seconds, the fighting was hand-to-hand. Gerber raced out of the bunker, joining the men on the wall. Smith followed him. Together they managed to rally the Vietnamese. Seeing the huge Americans out there with them inspired them. They fought harder. But there were too many of the VC. They began to take heavy losses. Gerber realized that they couldn't hold the wall.

But Gerber didn't have the problem that Bromhead had. There was a secondary line of defense among the bunkers and sandbagged buildings on the east side of the runway. He could abandon the wall and still prevent the VC from getting behind the defenders on the south and north.

Gerber left the wall and yelled into the bunker, "Destroy the weapon and fall back." He didn't have to give the order twice. To the men on the wall he yelled, "By section, fall back."

They had drilled the Vietnamese on this. But with the order, the courage of some of them broke. They fled. Others stood fast.

Smith dropped off his position, turned, and sprinted to the bunkers behind him, yelling for some of the Vietnamese to follow him. Once there, he tried to rally them, readying them for the assault that was going to come.

Gerber saw that the resistance on the wall had effectively ended. He yelled, "Everyone. Fall back! Fall back!"

He left his position, watching the wall, firing his rifle from the hip, only trying to slow down the advance of the VC. He saw a couple fall. One raced at him, his bayonet out. Gerber easily parried the enemy's thrust and shot him at close range.

"Over here, Captain," called Smith.

Gerber turned and saw the sergeant standing surrounded by defenders. Gerber tried to force his way to Smith, knowing that he had found the backup communications.

On the north side of the camp, the 60mm mortar pits were now in danger. Gerber called them, and ordered them to start dropping willy pete, charge one, practically on the east wall. He knew that it was dangerous dropping it that close, but they were being overrun.

The fighting again became hand-to-hand. Gerber was using his bayonet to keep the VC away from him. For a moment he was too busy to think of anything else. It was almost as if the Viet Cong knew who he was and were all trying to kill him. But Smith, with a small group of Vietnamese, moved forward, surrounding the captain. While he was still alive, Smith was determined to make sure that Gerber stayed alive.

Gerber, realizing that he was momentarily protected, picked up the field phone near him. In one horrifying second, he realized that it was dead. He was no longer able to talk to Bocker.

In the group of men around him, Gerber found Smith. In his ear, he yelled, "I've got to get to the commo bunker."

He wanted to offer an explanation, but there was no time, and Smith didn't really expect one. He organized the Vietnamese, and they began fighting their way toward the commo bunker, about thirty yards away.

As they moved, the group shrank as men were killed and wounded. There were only six of them left when they got to the bunker. Bocker was in the doorway, trying to cover them.

"The fast movers," yelled Gerber.

"Almost here."

Gerber pushed past Bocker, found the radio, and picked up the mike. "Stinger aircraft. This is Zulu Six."

"Stinger One One. We are less than one out. Where do you want it?"

The last time Gerber had seen the east wall, it was on fire, thanks to the willy pete that the mortar crews had dropped on it. He said, "North to south on the east side of the camp. East side is marked by numerous fires. Be advised that we have lost the east wall. I say again, we have lost the east wall."

There was a moment of silence, and then, "Roger. Understand north to south. East wall lost."

"Roger." Gerber dropped the mike and ran back outside.

A hundred VC, maybe twice that, had climbed the wall and were attacking the defenders. Instead of hitting the whole line at once, they were concentrating on one bunker, trying to take it. Gerber pointed this out to Smith, and they turned as much of their remaining firepower as possible toward the enemy there.

Overhead, there was a roar from a jet engine, and on the ground, only ten or twenty yards from the east wall, there was a flaming explosion, as the first of the napalm hit. It was followed, seconds later, by another. A minute after that, there were two more, and then two more.

Resistance by the VC in the camp seemed to stiffen, and then fade. Seeing this, Gerber ordered Bocker to stop the mortars and started a counterattack that forced the enemy back to the wall. At the same time, the jets were making strafing runs, hitting the two companies that the VC had held back, hoping that a heavy reserve would crack the east wall. The jets made sure they didn't have the chance.

Inside the central bunker, Gerber picked up the field phone and gave the mortar pits new instructions. He ordered the sixties to begin dropping HE in the paddies east of camp and had the eighty-ones start throwing stuff a little farther, hoping to break up any attempts by the VC to rally and attack again.

Bocker told him that the jets had expended everything they had brought and would be going back to rearm. Another flight of three would be on station in a few minutes.

To the east, Gerber could see little. Smoke from a hundred fires obscured the view. But there was now little incoming fire. He found Sully Smith, kneeling near a badly wounded Vietnamese corporal, trying to stop the bleeding from a chest wound. He said to him, ''I've got to try to find out how the rest of the camp is making out. Be at the commo bunker.''

Without looking up, Smith said, ''Yes sir.''

Around him he could see the Vietnamese checking the bodies of the VC, making sure that they were dead. They were picking up the dropped weapons and looking for booby traps and mines that the VC who had gotten inside the camp might have spread around. He could see that the majority of the force was back on the wall. Little was left of the bunkers. Most were pouring smoke from fires started by the willy pete.

Gerber ran back to the commo bunker. Bocker, rifle in hand, was still in the doorway, watching. From inside, Gerber could hear the static from the radios, but no one was talking on them.

He climbed to the top of the bunker, realizing that there were no incoming mortars. He found the field phone, or rather the remains of it. It had been hit a couple of times by small-arms fire. He didn't understand how that could have happened.

In the north, it seemed calm. In the west, he could see fires burning, and an occasional red tracer lace outward.

He didn't see any incoming fire, however. It was the same in the south. Some outgoing firing, but nothing apparent coming in. Gerber climbed down and walked around to the commo bunker doorway.

"Nearly sunup, Captain," said Bocker.

Gerber glanced at his watch and saw that the crystal had been shattered sometime during the night. "What time you got?"

"Quarter to five."

Gerber stared at the commo sergeant. "My God, you don't think it's over?"

"Getting awful late, Captain. Charlie needs time to get out of here since he hasn't taken the camp."

Gerber walked into the bunker so that he could talk to Stinger Operations. He wanted to make sure that there was another airstrike coming. He didn't care if there were no VC around the camp anymore. He wanted the airplanes out there because he knew that he could find them a target.

CHAPTER 16

In the east, there was a smudge of light on the horizon that suggested that dawn was near. Gerber, carrying a new field phone, had climbed to the top of the commo bunker. Now he was surveying the area to the east, looking for a hint that the VC were still out there. But all he could see, through the smoke of the fires on the east wall and the burning trees and elephant grass in the distance, were the bodies of the two VC battalions that had tried to take that side of the camp.

The only movement he could see was along the ruins of the bunkers as the medics worked their way among the wounded, trying to save as many lives as they could. There was no sound there, no firing, only the moans and cries of the wounded. Smoke hung heavy over the entire camp.

To the north, there was nothing to see. It looked like new. There had been no assault against the bunkers there.

Across the runway, which had been so badly mortared that it would be impossible to land aircraft, the west line was quiet too. Even with the binoculars and the increasing light from the rising sun, it was hard to see anything. The ground, almost all the way to the runway, was littered with bodies. Fires spotted the line there, and in the front of it there were more bodies: another VC battalion that had destroyed itself trying to breach the wall.

199

And in the south, there was more of the same. Bodies. Burning bunkers. The cries of the wounded. Gerber knew that Minh was struggling to put the line back into some kind of order, because if there was a final assault, it almost had to come from that direction. There was good cover, and a quick escape route in the river. Charlie could use it for cover until it was dark again.

Sergeant McMillan pulled himself to the top of the bunker and said to Gerber, "Bad news, sir. Kepler was bayoneted. The blade missed everything vital, but he lost a lot of blood. Clarke took some shrapnel in the arm. Lieutenant Bromhead was hit in the back, and I've patched him up. He's still on the west wall. Kittredge is still unconscious."

Gerber lowered his binoculars and then sat down. He stared to the east, but didn't speak. All he could think of was that he had started to build a camp with a team of eleven men. Now one of them was dead, several had been wounded, and one of them was in Saigon because he was having a hard time coping with the deaths of his LP team. Not a very good track record.

The field phone was ringing and Gerber answered it. Bocker told him that the fast movers would be on station in about five minutes. Gerber said, "Any reports from Minh or Bromhead?"

"Negative on the south. Lieutenant Bromhead said that he thought there was movement far to the west, as if the VC are trying to get back across the border."

"No incoming fire?"

"No sir."

"Troops massing? Anything?"

"Nothing. Nothing at all."

"Okay." Gerber hung up, looked around one last time, and then dropped to the ground. In the commo bunker, he picked up a PRC-10 and told Bocker that he was going to the west wall.

Bromhead and Fetterman were still there, watching the

open ground in front of them. Vietnamese and Tais were helping the wounded and picking up the weapons scattered around the area.

"Anything happening out there?" asked Gerber.

"No sir," said Bromhead. "Some movement about a thousand meters out, but I don't think it will threaten the camp."

Gerber saw that the back of Bromhead's jungle jacket had been ripped out. He said, "You okay?"

"Sure." Bromhead nodded. "Just a little shrapnel. The doc got it out and bandaged me up. I'll be okay."

By looking around, Gerber could tell that the fight on the wall had been close. There were piles of bodies around the bunkers. Dozens of bodies were lying in the wire, around the pungi moat, and on the earthen embankment. Behind him were more bodies.

Just as everywhere else in the camp, there were fires: fires from the mortar rounds, fires ignited by the tracers, and fires started by Fetterman and his flamethrower.

The PRC-10 came alive. "Zulu Six, this is Stinger Two Five."

"Roger, Two Five. This is Six. We need you to hit the west side of the camp, about a thousand meters out. Target is fleeing toward the border. Under no circumstances are you to cross the border. I say again. Do not cross the border."

"I understand. Can you mark target?"

"That's a negative."

"Roger, Six. We'll take care of it."

Gerber sat down to watch. The jets made one pass, flying east to west as a spotting run. They broke to the north, turned, and came back, north to south. The sky was now gray, and Gerber saw two large cylinders tumble from the aircraft. They exploded into flame when they hit.

The second made its run, and then the third. Each made another pass, dropping napalm, and then began strafing runs. With the enemy out of sight, all they could do was watch the show.

Bocker walked up, stood and watched, and then said to Gerber, "Captain, I've just talked to Colonel Bates. He's inbound now. Requested permission to land."

Gerber stood up. "I suppose I should go talk to him." He turned to Bromhead. "Keep me posted. I think we've weathered this storm."

As they started back across the camp, Gerber saw just how bad the damage was. Nearly every structure had been hit. Some of them had burned to the ground. Others had been riddled by small-arms fire and shrapnel. The sandbags protecting some building had been so shot full of holes that most of the sand had spilled out. The ground was littered with debris. It was almost as if there wasn't a camp left. Only the ruins of one.

In the commo bunker, Gerber talked to Bates, suggesting that it might be better to wait an hour or so before landing. There was still movement west of camp, and Gerber thought that they might still take some incoming harassment fire.

Bates responded, "Negative, Zulu Six. We will land at your location unless you are still under attack."

Gerber rogered and told him to land on the helipad near the northern end of the runway. Everywhere else was too badly shot up.

He had just signed off when there was a new message. "Zulu Six, this is Big Green Six. Understand we are to land on the November side of the Romeo Whiskey."

Gerber looked at Bocker. "I think he means the north side of the runway," Bocker suggested.

"He's doing more to confuse us than the VC." On the radio Gerber said, "That's a roger."

"Understand you will be at pad when we shut down."

Gerber sighed and looked at the ceiling. Over the radio he said, "Roger."

"Look at the bright side, Captain," said Bocker. "At

least he'll know that there are VC out there. Hell, they're lying all over the place. He can't claim that there are no enemy in the area.''

''He could always say they moved into the area because we did.''

''So what? Part of this is to meet the enemy, and if we can make him come to us, it makes our job easier.''

''I don't think the general will see it that way. He'll still say that the camp should have been put somewhere else.''

From the outside they could hear the beat of helicopter rotor blades. Gerber said, ''That should be Bates. I guess I'll go out there and meet them.''

The north side of the camp looked as if it belonged somewhere else. It was nearly intact, having taken only a little incoming fire at the beginning of the assault. All Gerber had to do was look either right or left to have the impression changed.

Bates climbed out of the aircraft and said, ''Christ, that must have been close.''

''Closer than I care to admit. Nearly lost the east wall. They hit it with two battalions. The attack must have involved at least a whole ~~fucking~~ regiment, and maybe a reinforced whole ~~fucking~~ regiment. If they had gotten a couple of breaks, you could be talking to the new camp commander right now. A VC commander.''

Bates turned slowly, not believing what he was seeing. There were bodies everywhere. ''How many did you lose?''

''We're not sure yet. Haven't had a chance for a muster, but I think it was close to one hundred and fifty. About half our strength. No Americans killed but nearly all of them wounded, most of that slight.''

''Let's go check things out.''

''Can't. Crinshaw is on his way in and wants me to meet him here. Guess now he can't tell us that there are no VC around.''

Seconds later they heard another helicopter. Gerber pointed and they watched as the black speck became larger.

To Bates he said, "I wish you people had waited. We haven't sent out any patrols, so we don't know what's left around here. Charlie could have left a squad with a mortar to take out the wheels and news reporters who show up."

"You think that's a possibility?"

"Of course. Or he may have just cut out for the border."

Crinshaw's chopper came close, settled toward the ground, and landed in a whirlwind of dust and loose paper.

Captain Butolp, the general's aide, leaped clear of the helicopter, hit the ground, rolled two meters, and came up on one knee, his tommy gun ready.

Gerber looked down at the man and shook his head. "You're going to spoil the crease in your fatigues that way, Captain. We're pretty secure here now. Unless, of course, Charlie left a couple of snipers around."

The man looked uncertainly at Gerber from beneath the brim of his helmet, then got sheepishly to his feet.

After a moment three television newsmen, one carrying a camera, emerged from the helicopter, attired in helmets, flak jackets, and sports shirts. They were followed by General Billy Joe Crinshaw, his chrome-plated .45-caliber Colt's Government Model pistol in his hand.

When he saw Crinshaw, Gerber said, "We got your body count for you, General. We don't have the exact number yet, but you can still see them hanging in the wire."

Crinshaw shot him an angry look but didn't say anything as the network news personality shoved a microphone into Gerber's face. "Excuse me, who are you?"

Gerber, still wearing his torn and bloodstained fatigues, said, "Excuse me. Who are you?"

"Peter Fleming, CBS News. Who are you?"

Crinshaw, pushing his way forward, said, "This is Captain Mack Gerber, my number-one camp commander." Looking at Gerber, he said, "What's the tactical situation here, Mack?"

Rolling his eyes at Bates, Gerber said, "Well, General, the tactical situation here ~~sucks~~."

Fleming shoved the mike back into Gerber's face and said, "Can you be a little more specific, Captain."

"We got hit by a large force of VC last night and managed to repel the attack. Now, if you'll excuse me, I have wounded men to look after."

Crinshaw pushed himself between Gerber and the camera again. "Let the captain go for now, boys. You all will get another chance to talk to him later. Right now, he and I got a lot of important work to do.

"Captain Butolp, you want to take these fine gentlemen of the press, let them get some shots of the camp, let them get some shots of the dead Cong, and then take them over to the team bunker and get them some coffee. Colonel Bates and I will be over there just as soon as we find out just exactly what the situation is here."

"The team bunker was destroyed last night," said Gerber.

He waved Gerber to keep quiet. To Butolp he said, "Damn it, man, find them some coffee somewhere."

Crinshaw threw an arm around Gerber's shoulder and started walking him away from the press. "Listen, son, you got to be more careful about how you talk to the media boys. After all, we're going to be on the network news tomorrow night. You don't want to upset the press. A thing like that can hurt a man's career. Know what I mean?"

"Oh, yes sir. I know exactly what you mean."

As they walked toward the commo bunker, stepping around the bodies that were in the way, Crinshaw kicked at one or two and said to Gerber, "Where are the weapons?"

"We pick those up as fast as we can. Don't want to leave them around, just in case. By the way, Charlie sometimes boobytraps the bodies so it isn't a good idea to kick them."

"Where's the exec?" asked Crinshaw, changing the subject.

"Still on the west wall. We had an air strike in there. Last movement we saw was there. Oh, and we were damned careful not to drop anything into Cambodia. They might be sitting in there lobbing shells at us, but we sure as hell won't fire back and break the rules."

Again, Crinshaw didn't respond to Gerber's criticism of official policy. He just walked on slowly, looking at the smoking ruins and the crater-filled runway.

"We lost a lot of equipment last night. Most of it destroyed by the enemy, but some of it we blew up when we lost the east wall. Didn't want Charlie turning it on us."

Quietly Crinshaw said, "Give Colonel Bates a list of everything you need."

At the commo bunker, Gerber saw McMillan talking to Bocker. As they walked up, McMillan said, "Sir, I think we better evac Sergeant Kepler. That wound of his was deep. I don't know how he stayed on his feet as long as he did. In fact, we need to get quite a few people evaced. Kittredge too."

Bates broke in. "You can send some out on my aircraft if you need to. I can find a way back to Saigon."

"Yes sir. That will help."

McMillan looked meaningfully at Crinshaw.

"I'd like to give you mine too, Sergeant, but the press has to get back to Saigon to file their story."

"Yes sir," said McMillan levelly. "I can see how that would take priority, sir. That's all right. Sergeant Bocker has already called for a medivac and it should be here inside an hour. I suppose that most of them should make it. After all, they are only Vietnamese, sir. Yes sir, I can see where the press is more important." His face flushed with anger.

"What about Bromhead and some of the others?" asked

Gerber, trying to protect his sergeant from Crinshaw's possible wrath.

"Mostly just lacerations. We've got enough medicine now that I should be able to fight infection. If we can spare him, I think maybe Lieutenant Bromhead ought to be treated in Saigon for a day or two."

"Maybe later this afternoon, but not now."

"Yes sir. I can arrange to have the most seriously wounded taken out on Colonel Bates's aircraft."

"All right. Keep me posted. Oh, and see if Sergeant Bocker can get word to Lieutenant Morrow in Nha Trang that we weathered the storm. We'll be touring the base." Gerber emphasized the word "touring" sarcastically.

Lieutenant Minh was sitting on the remains of the central bunker on the south wall, not doing much of anything. Around him, the Vietnamese were halfheartedly watching the wires, but there was no movement out there. Charlie had been so badly chopped up that he couldn't even drag away the dead. And from the moaning, there were quite a few wounded left behind.

Crinshaw walked up to the Vietnamese officer and said, "Don't you think you should get some help out there to those wounded men?"

Minh stood up, favoring his right leg. From the bloodstain on it, it was obvious that he had been hit. To Crinshaw he said, "Not until my own men are taken care of, old boy. Wouldn't be proper form to help the enemy before we take care of our own."

They finished the tour quickly, after that. Crinshaw had seen all that he really wanted to see. The camp was a shambles, and he figured that now was the time to abandon it. He could force the issue, saying now that the VC had been defeated, the camp would be of more use near Tay Ninh. Besides, he could also argue that the camp was in an indefensible location. The network news broadcast would establish the tremendous amount of damage the communists had been able to inflict. Charlie had given him the excuse that he needed.

They turned and started walking back toward the northern end of the perimeter. Lying in the dirt, Crinshaw saw a Russian pistol, near the outstretched hand of a dead Viet Cong officer. He picked it up and said, "Guess I got myself a souvenir."

Gerber started to protest that it belonged to those who had defended the camp, but Bates cut him off, saying, "It will look good on your office wall, General. With a big plaque telling that it was captured in the battle here."

"Of course. Of course."

Back at the helicopter, the newsmen were milling around, glancing at their watches and looking nervous. "General, are we going to be leaving soon?" asked Fleming. "We need to get back to Saigon if we're going to get the film on the noon plane."

"Be with you all in just a minute." Crinshaw waved. He turned to Bates and Gerber. "You know, Plans and Operations back at MAAG, is going to be asking a lot of tough questions about the continuing viability of this command. What would be you boys' recommendations as to what we ought to do now?"

Gerber shrugged. He knew what he had to do. He had to rebuild. To start over. It was the only thing to do. In the battle, he had broken the back, at the very least, of a hard-core regiment, possibly a reinforced regiment. It would be awhile before Charlie could get a new force into the area to oppose him, and Gerber could use that time to make the camp so strong that a division would be needed to overrun it. Helplessly he looked at Bates.

To Bates, Crinshaw's question was more than pointless. He knew exactly what they had to do. It was so obvious that even the lowest-ranking private, in the darkest, safest bunker in Saigon, had to know what they should do now. Out loud, Bates said, "Why, I'd suggest that we rebuild the camp, General. Otherwise Charlie wins anyway."

Fleming, who had sneaked up behind them in order to hurry the general along, overheard Bates's statement. "Say, that's really good. Can I quote you on that? Would you mind saying that for the camera?"

Bates and Gerber exchanged disbelieving looks. Then Bates smiled slowly. "Why, of course, Mr., ah, Fleming, wasn't it? We're always glad to assist the press in whatever way we can. I'll be happy to repeat that statement for you, on camera, exactly word for word."

GLOSSARY

AC—Aircraft Commander

AK-47—Assault rifle normally used by the North Vietnamese and the Viet Cong.

AO—Area of operations.

ARVN—Army of the Republic of Vietnam. A South Vietnamese soldier. Also known as Marvin Arvin.

BAC SE—Vietnamese for doctor.

BAR—Browning automatic rifle.

BODY COUNT—The number of enemy killed, wounded, or captured during an operation. Used by Saigon and Washington as a means of measuring progress of the war.

BOOM BOOM—Term used by the Vietnamese prostitutes in selling their product.

CARIBOU—Cargo transport plane.

CHICOM—Chinese communist.

CHOLON—The Chinese section of Saigon.

CLAYMORE—An antipersonnel mine that fires seven hundred fifty steel balls with a lethal range of fifty meters.

DAI UY—Vietnamese army rank the equivalent of captain.

DSC—Distinguished Service Cross, the nation's second-highest award.

E-TOOL—An entrenching tool. A small folding shovel.

FCT—Fire control tower.

FIVE—Radio call sign for the executive officer of a unit.

GARAND—The M-1 rifle that was replaced by the M-14. Issued to the Vietnamese early in the war.

HE—High-explosive ammunition.

HOOTCH—Almost any shelter, from temporary to long term.

INCREMENTS—Removable propellant charges attached to a mortar round.

LAMBRETTA—Small, open vehicle used for transportation.

LIMA LIMA—Land line. A field telephone.

LLDB—Luc Luong Dac Biet. The South Vietnamese Special Forces.

LP—Listening post. A position outside the perimeter manned by a couple of people to give advance warning of enemy activity.

LZ—Landing zone.

M-14—Standard rifle of the U.S., eventually replaced by the M-16. It fired the standard NATO round: 7.62mm.

MAAG—Military Assistance Advisory Group, finally disolved in May 1964.

MACV—Military Assistance Command, Vietnam, replaced MAAG in 1964.

MEDIVAC—Also called Dustoff, a helicopter used to take the wounded to the medical facilities.

MPC—Military Payment Certificate—paper money, sometimes called monopoly money—issued in lieu of regular currency. Denominations started with the nickel.

NAPALM—Jellied gasoline used in bombs and flamethrowers that sticks to the surface it burns. Name derived from *na*phthenic and *palm*itic acids.

NCO—A noncommissioned officer. A noncom. A sergeant.

NOUC-MAM—A strong-smelling sauce used by the Vietnamese.

NVA—North Vietnamese Army.

PRC-10—Man-portable radio.

PUFF—Or Puff the Magic Dragon. C-47 aircraft carrying a multitude of weapons, later designated as Spooky.

PUNGI STAKE—Sharpened bamboo hidden to penetrate the foot, sometimes dipped in feces.

RF—Local military forces recruited and employed inside a province. Known as Regional Forces.

RPD—Soviet light machine gun, 7.62mm.

SAPPER—An enemy soldier used in demolitions. Uses explosives during attacks.

SATCHEL CHARGE—Explosive charge fitted with a handle for easy carrying and throwing.

SEABEES—Naval construction battalions used to build nearly everything imaginable.

SIX—Radio call sign for the unit commander.

SKS—Soviet-made carbine.

SMG—Submachine gun.

TAI—A Vietnamese ethnic group living in the mountainous regions.

THREE—Radio call sign of the operations officer.

THE WORLD—The United States.

TWO—Radio call sign of the intelligence officer.

VC—Viet Cong, called Victor Charlie (phonetic alphabet), or just Charlie.

VIET CONG—A contraction of Vietnam Cong San (Vietnamese Communist.)

VNAF—South Vietnamese Air Force.

WILLY PETE—WP, white phosphorus, called smoke rounds. Used primarily for incendiary and casualty effect, and for marking targets.

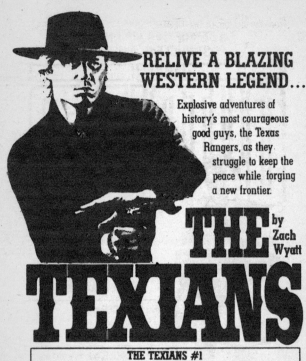